Michael Cole, although sem[illegible] makes body jewellery for a firm in Bristol, where he lives. He has always had an interest in competitive horse riding and combines this interest with his hobby of coin-detecting in the wilds of Wiltshire.

Spring Moon over Badminton

Michael E Cole

To
Pat
Best Wishes For
The Future
Mike

Dragon Fly
Press

First published in 2002 by Dragon Fly Press
1 Berkeley House, Berkeley Rd
Staple Hill, Bristol BS16 5HS

Distributed by Gazelle Book Services Limited
Falcon House, Queen Square
Lancaster, England LA1 1RN

British Library Cataloguing in Publication Data
A catalogue record for this book is available from the British Library

ISBN 0-9541925-0-8

Typeset by Amolibros, Watchet, Somerset
This book production has been managed by Amolibros
Printed and bound by T J International, Padstow, Cornwall, UK

Acknowledgements

Jane Holderness-Roddam (Chairman, British Eventing) for having the patience of a saint.

Christina MC Quillan, who rides like a dream.

And not forgetting Windsor Heights, the proud eight-year-old stallion from West Kington Stud.

Katrina

Katrina Chambers lay on her back completely naked. Every morning for the last week she had inspected her almost flawless body with a critical eye. Not for her the English white rose skin—her face was deeply tanned by the wind and sun, and the rest of her body a perfect bronze to match. Only the scar that ran from her right eyebrow into her hair marred her almost perfect features. The hand mirror was slanted to catch the light as she brushed down her blond fringe to cover the blemish. Only when she was completely satisfied that every part of the whiteness was hidden, did she sweep back the rest of her hair and expertly split and plait the strands into a horse rider's pony-tail. Most days or whenever possible, Katrina, or Katy to her friends, would have a leisurely breakfast with her mother and father, and around eight-thirty drive the short journey out to the stables. This day was special: it was Saturday, the one morning that she had prayed for all week, now it was here and her whole body was quivering with excitement and anticipation. How many times over the last few days had she hugged the pillow savagely to her as if it was his form, and bit her lip in sexual frustration? Playing with her over-stretched emotions had only increased the pressure of waiting throughout the last few days for this glorious awakening. Time was moving her inexplicably forward in a dizzy spiral towards meeting the stranger in her father's valley. The noisy chatter from a pair of magpies fluttering around the branches of the large sycamore tree broke in obtrusively on her concentration. Katrina turned her head towards the noise and was surprised to note that the earlier greyness of sky had already been replaced by a light blue sheen. The beginning of May was starting with a fine sunny day, already beginning to unfold rapidly. Then the loud protesting warning cry from a blackbird as it was unceremoniously hassled from its territory by one of its large black and white neighbours acted as a starting pistol for her.

Quickly she swung her feet onto the carpet, and, as her lithe body moved forward, the piece of paper which was lying on her pillow was brushed onto the floor. Katrina trembled before bending and retrieving the folded foolscap from under the table; there had been no troubled dream in the night to haunt her, not like most of the other nights since the invitation had come. Sometimes she was a small child, tottering towards the butterfly resting on the bright yellow flower near the water. Or she saw a hand reaching out desperately to snatch the bent-over toddler from danger, only to clutch thin air as horse and rider seemed to hang in the air above them. Either of the two would find her in a bath of sweat when she awoke, as she had been in her nightmare—the water that had cascaded over her as horse and rider parted company and smashed down into the lake close by was still with her. Katrina shuddered before folding neatly the prestigious invitation to ride at Badminton, then kissed it gently before placing it on the dressing table.

Fifteen minutes later she was purposely striding up through the valley close to her home taking as many short cuts as possible. She left a clear trail of dew-sodden, now trampled grass as she diverted from the hard brown meandering path to gain time. Usually, a short, fast drive in her sports car was her routine, since she could arrive at the stables within minutes. Katrina gave a sigh as she closed another gate behind her; today was different, and for her plan even to have the remotest chance of working, walking was the only option. Across the stream on her left loomed a large impregnable mass of interwoven blackberry and short hawthorn scrubs, three to four metres high and over ten metres in diameter. Pausing in her stride she looked at her watch—the hands showed six-fifty-nine. Katrina hesitated, then stopped. The temptation to cross the small bridge and crawl into the tunnel that penetrated the dome was tempting. But she had already noted the long wake of trampled grass behind her, and for someone to follow her trail or accidentally stumble on her secret hiding place of many years seemed the height of stupidity. Not when, in the near future, she could indulge safely from preying eyes within its hidden beauty with the one she loved. Kelly was waiting and expecting her, although this morning Katrina was lethargic about the business of saddling him ready to ride. There were more important things on her mind, and he could sense it. The large horse was on his toes, dancing, and his rider realised that even to contemplate thinking of anything else except having complete control would court disaster. Over the last weeks she had honed him to perfection, now he was ready for the biggest battle of his life, and uncannily he seemed to understand that day was drawing rapidly nearer.

Rodrick

Youngest son of Lord Johngowen, family home Gowen Estate, Wiltshire, comprising one mansion with stables, eight tenant farms, and approximately twenty-six thousand acres. Other holdings in Hampshire, Dorset, Cornwall, plus tree plantations in Scotland. Large investments in tea companies, although now diversifying into electronics, and aviation. Wealth accumulated through Bristol Merchants and other sea-going ports. Rumours that the family dealt with the notorious Edward Teach, Bristol Pirate, not proven.

The tall, thin, and wiry Gowen estate manager kicked the wheel of the twin-engined Cessna savagely; the dull thud of leather on rubber brought an immediate muffed response from inside the plane. "Sir, if you keep shaking the blasted thing we will never sort out your fuel pump." The words were clear and precise, not the Scottish burr he was expecting, more Cockney London with just the right amount of respect—but also with the implied threat that interference would not be tolerated if they wanted to leave the Highlands this morning.

The pilot looked to the heavens for guidance as his passenger growled an unintelligible reply. Ten minutes or one hour—the time was unimportant now they were late, so he could expect a very unpleasant flight south.

Rodrick moved away from the plane slowly with one hand in his coat pocket, and as he walked almost in a circle his fingers clutched tightly a small velvet-covered box. Three days he had carried it with him; the ring was exquisite, rare Welsh Gold set with a diamond cluster, and he knew that it would fit perfectly, for her mother had managed to have her daughter's favourite ring sized secretly for him over two months ago. Always delays: instead of driving down to Cardiff and taking her with him, and giving her a tremendous surprise in the jewellers, he was forced to divert his journey to Scotland. Rodrick forced a grin. Already he had phoned and passed on a message to her mother that there had been a technical hitch, but he should arrive in Wiltshire around twelve and would call Katrina straight away. Just a quick glance at his Rolex watch showed seven-fifty-five; George her father would arrive from Manchester in the afternoon so there was no hurry really. The crisp twenty-pound notes ceased rustling as they were folded and placed back in his wallet; there was no need for any incentives, it would be to his advantage, he thought, if they were all together when he gave her this tremendously expensive token of his love. Rodrick grinned as he thought of the secret places he had never explored; their relationship over the years had been as brother and sister, almost as if he had replaced her brother Richard who had never returned from university but had joined the army those many years ago. They were well suited for each other, although a dark frown crossed his face: there was a faint chance that Katrina would make the Olympic squad, while he had not even been invited to compete for a place. There were no other suitors in her life—he had made sure of that; everyone knew that they were a couple, and now that she was twenty it was time that their platonic relationship was ended. Rodrick took out the engagement ring and looked at it closely. At least when Katrina was wearing the gold band she could not object to sex with him, since his intentions were strictly honourable, more so than others they both knew.

Bath or Westminster Abbey for the wedding—whatever they chose it would outshine any others this year; all Katrina had to decide was when.

The pilot looked wary as his boss started to walk briskly towards him, but was pleasantly surprised to see that he was smiling. "Come on, Bret, where can I find a good cup of coffee?"

James

The young man pulled the duvet over his head to keep out the noise of the cleaner, as his mother, as she did every Saturday morning, descended on the carpets with a vengeance.

Six-foot-four inches in height, weight hovering around the fifteen and three-quarter stone mark, mostly of solid muscle. With a shock of dark thick unruly hair that had defied all the efforts of skilled stylists to stay in any sort of presentable order.

Muffled sounds came from above his head as he tried to find the gateway back to the sexual fantasy world he had been enjoying before his abrupt awaking.

"Come on, get up, you've been drinking again!" his father called softly.

James grunted and turned over to face the window, then cursed as a bright shaft of sunlight bursting through the wide open curtains burned into his drink-fuddled brain. That was the finish of his escape from reality for this morning at least, as all sleep had vanished taking with it the girl who had been haunting him for the last few weeks. Groaning, he turned again as he realised that waking up was no improvement, as her sweetness had disappeared with the darkness leaving him with a throbbing headache.

John smiled as he looked down on his only son: he would be twenty-four in a couple of months, and his only interest seemed to be football, and drinking with his mates. The former he wholeheartedly agreed with, but lately on a Friday night he would come home loaded, not that he was any bother—except that he would come home in the early hours of the morning, and tease the dog, who would race from one end of the bungalow to the other, jumping up and growling like some small demented demon and enjoying every minute of his torment. The watcher moved closer to the bed, looking down on the large still figure, then frowned; there never seemed to be any members of the opposite sex in his life, and only his mother could get away with any teasing on this subject.

John moved closer. "James, James," are you coming with me this morning?" Then in a lighter tone, "It's a nice day."

The feigned half-sleeper opened one eye lid slowly, then the other more quickly as the cover was pulled back sharply.

Two dark deep blue eyes focused on the speaker; they were magic probes of light that seemed to encompass all who were within their range. Many a young female, and some not so young, were drawn by their welcoming beacon, only to find that although their hearts were stolen, the only return was friendship not love.

"Damn, your mother would have a fit if she knew you were in bed with your clothes on."

When James walked it was like a coiled spring; so fast could he cover ground that at one time a couple of years ago one of the local professional soccer teams was interested in his services as a goalkeeper. Sometimes he tried to analyse where his short spell at the club had gone wrong; it was not his ability on the field of play that was for sure, as they never lost a match. When he was dropped, for no reason in his opinion, it came hard. After waiting three weeks for a game, training became pointless, so he had joined his mates again and at the moment was playing better than ever. Unfortunately, or otherwise, depending on the mood he was in, most of the team used the local public house close to where he lived, playing darts, skittles, and, paramount, drinking large quantities of ale. Within walking distance, one for the road usually meant two or three for him, now he was trying desperately to pull himself out of his self-imposed stupor. Then he made his usual empty promise to himself that next time he would walk away—he felt awful. "Dad, go away," he croaked.

"Ten minutes or I'll tell your mother."

Blackmail now: "Okay, where are we going, Home Farm?"

He grinned slyly as his father answered in the affirmative.

Twice he had noticed the girl, once from afar over a month ago, as she had sat tall in the saddle and rode flat out over the wooden training fences dotted around the valley. Then again, only last Saturday, but much closer than before: this time as the large horse muzzled her closely, and her plaited pony-tail glistened against the sleekness of his neck, they made a perfect contrast. Although only a few yards away from her she had seemed completely oblivious of his presence, for all her attention was wasted on the damned four-legged critter. This had riled him at the time: he could have been just a wooden gate-post, a nonentity. This slight, whether in his opinion intentional or not, had festered and worried him over the past week. Although he knew that there was only a slim chance that the rider would be in the valley exercising the horse, or better still in the stable yard, every inch of his large muscular frame ached to be close to her. Although they had made no contact, he had secretly and intently watched every movement of her tall female form. His eyes had travelled upwards from the polished riding boots towards the slim waist, and lingered longingly on her firm buttocks, that under her over-stretched jodhpurs seemed to taunt him and lock his gaze forever. The girl had flicked her hair as if to brush away a near-flying insect, and as her hand stretched backwards she had half-turned towards him. James grinned as he remembered so clearly the sudden gust of wind that ruffed and moulded the green cotton riding shirt, profiling the hard firm breasts already heightened and hardened by her raised hand. Even then he knew he would die for her; his face was on fire as his lustful thoughts brought him out into a sweat. Then the girl's face came into full profile as she walked the horse around the yard. In that split second, as her sparkling green eyes locked with his, he knew that he was so deeply in love that if he could not fully have her for his very own, she would torment him for the rest of his life.

Feeling himself blush at the thoughts still tumbling around in his mind, he had hurriedly bent down and fumbled with his green wellington boots. This action had only sent more blood rushing to his head, making his face more crimson than ever. Feeling a fool and embarrassed, he had gone through the pretext of removing a stone from his sock as the now mounted rider came towards him. Not daring to look up, he had only heard the sharp click of hoofs on cobbles, and briefly tasted the bitter sweat smell of animal and girl all mixed together in one lethal cocktail as they slowly passed by. Now every moment that he was awake he had troubled thoughts and always dawn was the worst time! Or was it the best? One thing for sure: he could not ever remember when he had enjoyed so many sexual thoughts in the morning, for her shape and form tantalised him like a phantom.

"James, hurry up, what are you doing, dreaming?"

Kicking back the last of his restraint, he rolled onto the floor, pushed himself up and made for the bathroom in haste. Dreaming was he? This girl was for real!

John walked towards where his car was parked. There was no hurry as his reluctant companion would take more than enough time in joining him. Usually fifteen to twenty minutes was the norm, or sometimes half an hour if his son burnt his toast using the grill instead of the toaster, then had to scrape off the blackened crumbs or completely remake. Carefully he opened the boot and checked that the inside was clear; an old blanket lay across the vinyl covering giving a soft lining. Only when he was absolutely sure that there were no protrusion from under the cover did he safely stow his two five-hundred-pounds apiece coin detectors.

The buried-treasure seeker mentally went through his checklist. It was no good receiving a signal if you forgot the tool to dig for it. Not that James was very interested in whether they found anything or not; it was only his mother's sharp tongue that drove him out of the house on a Saturday morning. Very rarely they worked together on a weekend, but only if they had some printing to finish for a customer, or a machine to repair would they let that override their leisure time, so for the most part they managed to keep weekends free. John scratched his head, then frowned as he tried to work out why James had asked if he was going to Home Farm for the morning. The most obvious answer was probably that the grass would be very short and easy to work because of the multitude of sheep that roamed over the valley. Within half an hour, if the weather was right, he would lie down and go to sleep as he usually did.

Grinning, he looked at his watch. Only ten minutes had gone by: if he was going to be early it would be another fifteen at least in his state… .

The noise of the front door banging broke his concentration, and he watched in amazement as skipping down the steps of their bungalow came a large agile figure, now totally transformed from the bleary-eyed lump hiding under the duvet such a short time ago. Dressed in smart trousers and jacket, even his shoes were buffed and shining, and, not least of all, a tie adorned this apparition.

John was momentary lost for words. It was incredible! A few seconds later he managed to blurt out the first thing that came into his head, "You want dropping off somewhere? Somewhat early for the pub, even for you!"

James smiled warmly but declined to answer. If only he knew that twice in the past week he had drove close to the farm hoping to see her but to no avail. Each time he had worn a tie on the trip, so the combination that he was wearing now was already set out in the wardrobe waiting for him. "Come on, Dad, let's go, we don't have all day."

James wondered why this hobby of grubbing around in the dirt for odd coins of no particular value or pieces of metal smashed into unrecognisable shapes could hold such a fascination for his father. Whilst he could relate to the solitude of the valley with only the sheep for company, and immerse himself in the beauty of the many chequered greens of the landscape, to sweat in an oiled Barbour waterproof coat all morning was beyond him.

Shaking his head to clear away the effects of last night's revels, James reached for a cigarette then replaced the packet unopened. The driver, seeing the gesture, held out his hand. "Come on then, I'll have one even if you don't."

"Okay, hang on a minute, I'll light one up for you." Flicking the lighter, he applied the small flame, then drew deeply till the end glowed red, before passing it to his father. Then unconsciously he automatically lit one himself. Two puffs later he leaned forward and stubbed it out in the ashtray.

"More money than sense, you have," John chivvied as he swerved to miss the unconcerned hedgehog meandering across the empty road in front.

"No, just didn't feel like one." This was a lie, and he knew it; the girl whom he had never met was already taking over his actions.

Slowly they drifted down the single-track tree-lined road, then James' heart leapt, as into view away to the right, high on a promontory, came Home Farm. Then it sank in an instant as his father turned left, away from the place he desperately wanted to visit, driving instead towards the small village in the distance.

"Dad, why aren't we going up to the farm?"

"It's all right. Alan rents the land through the valley, so there's no problem."

A few minutes later they entered an open gate, and parked next to a large barn. "See that building, they do all the sheep-shearing in there."

James mumbled under his breath, not replying directly. He was looking across the large expanse of brown earth that shimmered in the morning sun and at the small dust clouds swirling in the hollows mocking him. Looking back towards the farm, then turning so that he could see the roof-tops in the distance, he tried to calculate the time it would take to walk around this obstacle.

"Coming?" The words broke in on his concentration.

Swearing under his breath, he picked up his detector and reluctantly followed his father who was striding out across the barren field. Within minutes dirt and stones slipped unnoticed into his narrow-sided shoes making him wince at every step. The heat seemed to swell his neck, making him choke, and the distance from their objective did not seem to get any closer. Pride drove him forwards as out in front the striding figure seemed to make light work of the ploughed earth. James stopped, lifted up one foot and cleared out the debris, then the other.

"Blast, I must be out of my cotton-picking mind! What the hell am I doing here?"

Only the wind heard his cry, as his leader disappeared over the ridge from sight.

Reaching his goal at last, the short green grass and the cool shade of a hawthorn bush, James crashed down in a crumpled heap.

After a while he regained his composure and begun to clean up his attire. Taking off his now soiled shoes and removing the small pieces that had hindered his passage, he was amazed to find a neat brown ring encircling his white socks. Smiling broadly and looking round furtively, he quickly turned them inside out and pulled them back over toes and feet still discoloured by the soil. Grabbing a handful of dock leaves he tried vainly to bring back some resemblance of a shine to his footwear, then gave up. Fully attired and standing up, he brushed himself down with green stained hands, then feeling the packet of cigarettes that bulged invitingly in his pocket, he took one out, and with a flick of his lighter fired one up.

"What the hell, no one can see me," he said out loud.

Then his eyes were drawn briefly, towards his father who was already sweeping the ground with slow rhythmic movements. James shook his head as he looked around, and finding a soft grassy knoll close by, he lay down, put his hands behind his head, and puffed contentedly looking directly at the blue sky above.

❦

The stable yard was a bustle of horses and riders back from their morning work-out. Katrina paused again from rubbing down Kelly her mount. Twenty times already in the last half an hour, she had looked across the expanse of grass towards the road. Then, when she saw the white car briefly as it turned away from the farm to disappear over the rise, her heart had skipped a beat. But now there was nothing. Why had it not turned across the cattle grid? The shape and colour were the same. It must be John, the man with the detector.

Only a few weeks ago when talking to Alan, the owner of the farm, she had asked casually, "Who were they?"

"From Bristol, John, that's his name." He paused. "Tony—I think that's his name—is his son, I think? Come on, I'll show you a few old horse brasses they have found."

Katrina remembered following him into the kitchen

and listening intently as he placed out on the table the assorted spoils.

Metal detecting: this was new to her. Spread out on show were a couple of Roman coins badly eaten away with corrosion and other odd bits of metal—at least, if, or when, they met, she would know what they were doing in the valley. Kelly nudged her, which brought her back to the present. Tony, if that was his name—how could she find out for sure? Katrina raised her hand towards a wisp of loose hair, and as her fingers lightly brushed her cheek a small tingling spread across one side of her face, giving her the sensation that someone else was caressing her. Again the nudge came, as if the horse knew that her thoughts were not for him alone as her eyes were drawn once more towards the valley. Patting his forelock, she whispered, "I love you so much, you silly horse."

Startled, Katrina jumped as someone touched her shoulder. Turning around quickly and trying to control her thoughts, she saw one of the other riders smiling.

"Badminton next week, hope you do well, good luck!" The girl turned away, not noticing the frown that settled on the bronzed face. Burying her head in the horse's neck, Katrina held on tightly as a cold chill ran up her spine.

Badminton: a vivid picture had come into her mind as high above her a horse and rider had parted company to crash down in a welter of spray. This was when she was a child, but the memory still lingered as if it was only yesterday. Now, in a few days' time, both would be tested to their limit. Katrina led the reluctant horse into the stall, as still frowning, she spoke softly: "Please, not Kelly, not Kelly," she pleaded.

Alan was calling from the farmhouse door. "Katrina, your mother wants to know if you would like her to come and give you a lift down home."

The frown was still on her brow, but she answered with alertness, "Tell her no thanks, I'll walk."

"Right, I'll tell her."

Alan watched as Katrina strolled purposely from the yard to disappear from sight. So intent were his thoughts that the telephone's muffed tones were almost completely forgotten.

Katrina increased her stride as in the distance rooks swirled above the trees. Someone was close to the valley. Bang! Bang! The unmistakable noise of a shotgun echoed around the slopes, and as the black cloud rose higher their frantic cries funnelled towards her.

"Damn." She lashed her boots savagely with the riding whip, then slowed her pace as the loud reports stirred her memory. How long ago was it, six months? Or almost a year that the family had gone up to London to visit her brother Richard as he lay wounded in hospital. That had been only a brief stay but the sight of him lying pale-faced and still had really shaken her up.

The most serious injury was a bullet lodged in his leg. There was no war on, not that she knew of, but as far back as she could remember he had always been in the army.

Ten years older than her, at first in the early years they had united as a family fairly often. Then his visits became less frequent. When he came there was plenty of laughter in the house and always a present for her. On rare occasions a lady friend would accompany him, every one of them different except all had long legs that, when she was younger, seemed to stretch ever upwards. Catherine her mother always protested every time Richard turned up, but he would give her a hug, then usher off his latest conquest to the spare room. Such sorties in the last couple of years were almost non-existent and his letters were very few and far between. She did miss tremendously the laughter and the chaos he caused when he came to visit.

"Hello, Kiddo, how's it going?" was his favourite expression. Three months ago at least was the last time he had turned up, unannounced as usual, and she remembered it well. There had been no noise to disturb the quiet of the house; to all intents and purposes there was no one except herself within the four walls. Walking unconcerned from the bathroom into her bedroom with only her bra and pants on and going towards the chair where her clothes lay folded tidily, there had been no rap to announce his presence, just a slight brush of his hand as it slid along the paint of the open door.

"Hello, K——, my god who is this vision?"

She had been startled and turned her head quickly; there eyeing her up and down stood her brother. Blushing scarlet, Katrina grabbed the towel that was laying on the bed to cover herself.

Richard had turned towards the door, but not before he had slapped her smartly on the back of her white cotton briefs. His parting words were: "My, my, I will give notice of my presence from now on. Mother is sure going to have trouble with you in the future." Then he had walked out laughing.

The crunch of gravel outside the front door sent her quickly to the window. Furtively pulling the drawn curtains slightly back, she watched as Richard strolled down towards the small bridge spanning the stream. Now the house was empty, there would not be any other intrusions, not yet at least.

Opening slightly her wardrobe door she had taken a brief glimpse of her reflection in the full-length mirror fixed inside. Then moving sideways she had leaned forward so that only her face was reflected back at her. Bright green eyes stared back at her, and the puckered mouth exposed neat white teeth. Feeling more daring, she opened the door more fully, exposing herself in complete profile. Turning slowly she looked critically at every aspect of her body, then a flush came to her face as she remembered her brother's gaze. Small shudders shook her as her hands brushed over silky skin moving upwards towards her moulded breasts; fingers cupped briefly and she felt her nipples harden as her hand rustled over silk-enclosed flesh.

The noise of a car door opening brought the tingling sensations to an abrupt halt. She felt flustered at the intrusion as the front-door key rattled in the lock and footsteps sounded in the hall. Quickly she fled into the bathroom, locked the door, and turned the hot tap on full as if to drown the beating of her heart.

"Katrina is that you?" It was her mother, but there was no way that she could answer, so choked up was she with emotion and fright.

Something was missing. Then it had come to her there was no sheen—all of her brother's girl friends seemed to have that glow.

Warm within her water cocoon she had tried to analyse this puzzle—older, more mature? This was not it, one was younger than herself and the sparkle was in her.

Sex? Maybe not, some of her room-mates at college had held her spellbound as, all huddled together in a group, she had listened to the their latest exploits, but they did not glow.

Anyway, out walking in the valley a few years ago, she had stumbled on a mating pair. Then the answer had come, not in flash of inspiration but by way of logical deduction. It was love, wholly and truly committed adoration for someone, that was the secret. The towel felt rough against her skin as she dried the places where the dampness lingered. For the first time in her life, she felt overwhelming physical desire.

The blast of a car horn made her jump. Katrina found herself in the middle of the road, so deep in thought that even the noise from the iron cattle grid across the entrance to the farm had not broken her concentration as she walked across. The driver gestured to his passenger, "Is that Katrina? Wonder what's the matter? She's usually so alert. Have you seen her ride that huge stallion, that horse puts the fear of god in me."

"Anything frightens you, I told you not to drive so fast around these lanes."

The girl heard the toot, toot, as the car passed behind her, but did not turn round. Across the green panoramic landscape rolling away into the distance, white sheep were scattered in their hundreds, with a few black ones mixed in as if by mischance.

Many times in the past she had stood silently just taking in the beauty of the view. But not now—far down the valley, where the trees blended together to form a canopy, came a flash, then another. High on the ridge towards the left it came again, the sun reflecting on the machine, and she knew that at least one of the detectors was sweeping diligently.

"Please let there be two of them, let him be here this morning."

Vaulting the stile she ran the first hundred yards, scattering the white and black fleeces who protested loudly at her intrusion. Katrina crouched down so that the sun angled over her head, then scanned all parts of the grass meadow stretching before her for any other movement.

"Why am I doing this? What's wrong with me?" Except in her heart she knew that the stranger was the only thing that really mattered in her life. While sitting rock solid on Kelly high above the dry stone walls she had followed the young man over a number of Saturdays, each time moving closer as her needs grew. Only once had they been very close. Feminine instinct told her that he was watching, but, passing close on her horse, there had been no contact. Something nagged deep in her thoughts, and as his shape and form manifested in her mind again she began to sweat. Katrina jumped, and put her hand over her mouth. "Oh no, it can't be!" Thinking back intently, she tried to visualise every detail for the one she was searching for.

Tony, is that his name? Not that it mattered; three months ago was the first time he had entered her life. From a crack in the stable door she had watched a young man wrestle with rubber Wellington boots while an older and impatient man had urged him to hurry up. Six foot at least with dark hair, even then he reminded her of someone. Now she knew for sure. Although the hair was different in style and colour it was him—my god, she was in love with her brother's image! Walking more slowly down the winding ribbon of bare earth path she tried to control her thoughts. There was no going back now, somehow everything else was of little importance. The last week had been difficult; each day had brought her nearer to the horse trials. She was a professional, and riders of her calibre had no other thoughts except to represent their country at the highest level. But these thoughts had completely deserted her—now all she could think about was the stranger in the valley. Would he come? How could she make contact? Even her mother had made the comment that she seemed nervous, unusual for her daughter. Every day she had worked with Kelly, honing each other's skills so that when she rode out they blended as one. Only when she was riding would the stranger fade back into the twilight of her thoughts, so giving her a short respite from his powerful influence over her. Each night his presence had magnified during the week of waiting. At first, only to touch his body and be held were all that she desired. Now she was completely wanton, hugging her pillow in front of the full-length mirror, completely naked, making lewd signs at her reflection. Katrina felt the blush rise quickly to her face as she shuddered with anticipation. The distance closed, as head down in deep thought she was unaware of the activity enacted high on the ridge a short distance in front.

James awoke with a start as a shadow passed over his face. Where was he? The combination of his ploughing through the soil coupled with the large amount of alcohol from the night's revels had taken their toll. John was standing over him, holding out a large mug of hot steaming coffee. "It's boiling, be careful." From his vantage point, he looked down at the perspiring figure. Crumpled trousers, stained shoes, and, not least, a tie still knotted around his throat. The sweat had dried in rivulets staining his face a motley colour. "My, what a sight you look."

James levered himself up on one elbow. Half on his side he scanned the valley away to the right, then he saw what he had dreamed of and which had tormented him day and night. Quickly scrambling to his feet, he grabbed the coin searcher with one hand, then pointed towards the village in the opposite direction with the other.

"I, um, I'm going to give it a go down by the stream, all right?"

John looked away to the left. "Okay, don't you want a drink first?"

There was no answer, and he watched in amazement as his son tried desperately to negotiate the grassy slope with slick soled shoes When the girl had come into view, James' only concern was to work out the angle of descent so that he would be waiting for her on the path below. If only she did not look up and see him, there was a possibility that the girl would believe that they had met by accident, not by his design.

John watched a hawk slowly drifting down the valley, then he saw her. "You crafty bugger, that's why you wanted to come this morning, suit and all. Well I reckon you've blown it this time, out of your class that one," he whispered out loud.

Katrina looked up; not twenty yards away directly in her path was what she had been seeking. Immediately her mouth dried, and she felt a fluttering inside her body such as she had never experienced before. Panic seemed to overwhelm her whole frame as if she was trapped. Her eyes searched frantically for a means of escape. High on the ridge stood the watcher, while to the right flowed the stream. She was trapped, closer now, much to close, she could almost hear him breathing.

"Morning, lovely day?"

Katrina nodded, then steeled herself to look directly

into the motionless Tony's face. What she noticed first was the large smile that stretched from ear to ear. His light blue eyes sparkled from the reflected sun, then seemed to change colour and draw her swiftly into their deep dark blue pools.

"Where's your horse?"

Katrina tried to reply, but her body felt limp and no sound would come out.

"My name is James, what's yours?" The words came out lightly and with it a grubby hand was held out towards her, then slightly withdrawn as the owner realised how dirty it was.

In a trance her own arm moved forward, and as her fingers touched the bare skin of his wrist, a bolt of lightning seemed to rocket upwards into her shoulder, then completely consume the whole of her body. Spellbound the words came out broken: "Kat, Kate, it's Katrina."

"Lovely name," he whispered, as her hand slipped into his as if it was the most natural thing to do. They were close now, and Katrina realised how tall and broad he was. There was no doubt in her mind why this dark handsome stranger of a few minutes ago had completely captivated her heart. The blue liquid molten water still held her captive and strange feelings of overwhelming desire began to manifest as the temperature in her body started to rise rapidly. Wonderful words of endearment, gentle caresses, his first soft kiss, then the powerful meaningful acts of passion, lovers completely and totally—all these thoughts were going around like a kaleidoscope. Could he read her thoughts? How great was his desire for her? How could she communicate that he had already stolen her heart, and that her body had overwhelmingly surrendered too. Although neither had moved their feet, the distance had closed considerably between them. Now only a centimetre separated her taut tingling breasts from the ridged muscles on his chest. James shuddered as the tension mounted, and as he shook himself every fibre in her body cried out for his arms to encircle and crush her to him, to alleviate both their pain.

"Katrina." The call was loud, and its sound bounced off the sides of the valley and echoed amongst the trees. They both instantly pulled away from each other at the intrusion.

"It's…it's my brother Richard," she gasped.

"Will I see you again?" James forced out the words quickly as the girl started to run.

Without turning round she called back over her shoulder, "Maybe, yes, yes."

"When?" he screamed desperately at the fleeing shape, but the distance was far beyond the sound of his voice.

Richard caught the flying figure of his sister and swung her around easily. Then he saw the joy on her face, cheeks glowing as if on fire, panting as if she had run a mile, not the hundred yards or so to him. Katrina was physically very fit due to the constant working out with the horses, lean and supple but very strong, so the short distance to him would not have caused this radiant glow. Dropping her lightly on her feet he pulled her close to his body so that her face was buried in his neck, then his trained eyes scanned the copse from where his sister had run. Distortion broke the pattern of light and shade of the bushes, moving ever upwards at the edge of the small wood. Richard grinned: you naughty girl! Then he knew that all her exuberance was not for him alone, he had on this occasion to share it with another.

2

Pushing her back and holding tightly on to her shoulders, he said, "Kid, have I got news for you!"

Katrina caught the tone of his voice, happy like in the earlier years, brass buttons shining, peaked hat set firmly on his head. He was her hero.

"I'm getting married."

"When?" came her weak reply.

"Two weeks."

"Who is it? Will the wedding be in London or the local church?" Katrina expected her brother to point towards the small village church, but he shook his head.

"Joe, that's her name, Josie really. You will like her, she's smashing, and by the way, Kiddo, we are getting hitched in Barbados."

The last few words struck her rigid. Feeling a lump come into her throat she stammered, "B…b…but I won't be there?"

"Yes, you will, all of us are going, it's all arranged."

"But it's your honeymoon."

Richard laughed out loud, and hugged her more tightly as they reached the entrance to the valley. Katrina's head buzzed like a hive of bees; all she wanted to do now was hide in her room alone.

Then he said it, as if her mind was not already emotionally in turmoil and confusion. "What more could a man ask for than both of his loves on his honeymoon?"

Katrina started to cry, small tears at first, then larger ones began to run down her face and, sobbing uncontrollably, she pulled away and ran towards the safety of the house.

Another stranger was standing at the gate, short in stature with dark hair. Catherine her mother was in deep conversation with her, and Katrina knew at once it was Josie but almost pushed past the two of them without a word, her tear-streaked face still running with water. Making for the open front door in haste then mounting the stairs two at a time, she dived full-length onto her bed and with clenched fists beat at the pillows, at the same time pressing her face into them to try and stop the waterfall.

All her built-up emotions had welled up in a final volcanic eruption—the morning had just been too much.

Richard winced as the stone rolled under his foot and his calf muscle knotted tightly. Bending down, he rubbed it gingerly trying not to pressurise the blue scar that disfigured his leg. The bullet had entered and lodged in the bone. The wound had been a blessing in one way, for no more would he be dropped into unknown territory, and, best of all, he had met Joe. Now he was confined to sifting information, either sent or brought back from his former colleagues still on active duty, but he missed the danger and excitement.

Slowly the vehicle came down the slope towards the bent figure, the driver nudged his passenger. "That's Richard Chambers in the road, isn't it?"

"That's him, wonder what's the matter with that family today? You must find out."

Still rubbing his leg as best he could, he arrived at the gate of the house still limping as the car passed by, its occupants waved a greeting. Josie did likewise although she did not know who they were. Catherine called to her son, but he knew what was coming and pressed a finger to her lips. "It's all right, our Kiddo is just fine, Mother, she is happy."

"How can Katrina be happy rushing into the house like that, she look devastated—come on, tell me."

"Mother, there is nothing to tell, I know from experience our Kid is great."

Then he winked at both of them, stuck his hands in his pockets and walked off whistling up the stairs.

Josie saw the look on his face and had known in an instant what ailed the upstairs resident. Inwardly she smiled as the memories came back to her of when she had first met her future husband.

Over many months in the London Hospital she and her team had nursed him from the time when he had first arrived on a stretcher covered in bandages. Most of the injuries were just flesh wounds, but the bullet lodged in his leg was serious; septicaemia was always a possibility as the lead had been embedded for a number of days.

Over the next few weeks Richard had grown stronger and his family had travelled from Wiltshire to visit. The operations on his leg were a complete success, although he complained bitterly that the bullet they had taken out was not his to keep.

Then his pals descended like locusts onto the ward; chattering to the nurses, and in general causing chaos everywhere, they would arrive four or five at a time and with them came much laughter.

Richard and she had grown close while he was on her ward. He had told her of their large house tucked away in a small village and of his kid sister of whom he was very proud, also of his mother and father, and how sometimes he would board a transport plane that would fly him to places anywhere in the world. As they took off he could sometimes see the house in the hollow, and he would try to visualise what they were doing at that particular moment. Josie brushed her hair absentmindedly as the memories came back in sequence. There had been no warning, her patient was safely tucked up in bed when she had left her shift that evening, but when she had arrived in the morning he had gone. There had been no letter left for her, not even his telephone number that he had promised faithfully.

Three weeks later after his spiriting away from the

hospital, he had returned holding a large bunch of flowers. Bursting into the ward he had marched straight up and thrust them at her, and in one breath said, "Joe, let's go out this evening, don't say no, please."

Joe was it?—not ward sister, or even Josie; walk into your life, unburden yourself, then disappear, and turn up when it suits you. Funny thing was, her answer just came out without any reservations at all: "Ten o'clock outside, will that suit you?"

"Right." With that he was gone and only the swing doors betrayed his passage.

Looking back over her life before Richard had stepped into it, she wondered where all the time had gone. Leaving home in the north at eighteen, she had travelled down and taken a post in one of the training hospitals in London. There she had stayed in residence within the grounds; then, as she had progressed, a flat was shared with other nurses. Now she lived on her own, in a one-bedded small town house, a short distance from her profession.

That first night she was surprised to find a taxi waiting, when she had always surmised that Richard drove a car. They had been whisked away to a night-club, and when they had walked in all her feminine instincts told her that this was familiar ground for her escort. Slender female beauties with more than a knowing look nodded to Richard as they passed. One chap sitting at a table with two of the same stood up, waved, then sat down abruptly when he had seen her with him. They had danced and talked, and as the wine flowed the warmer and less uneasy she had become, pouring into attentive ears the story of her leaving Hull to seek her fortune in the capital. Then the pain of her father's death two years later at sea, and of her mother who died not long after, selling the house at a knock-down price to a cousin, and putting all of her energy into nursing.

Richard had let her talk. Not once did he break in on her chatter, and only when she dried up would he pour her some more wine and that seemed to make the words flow again.

Not on their first date, or any others since, did he divulge what he did for a living. She knew that he was in the armed forces and that was all she knew. Another thing nagged at her mind, although he had described the village where his family lived, and how on a hot summer's day if you were thirsty there was no pub, he had never actually told her its exact location. Castle Combe was mentioned with its quaint houses, and the almost tame trout in the clear water, and also Bath where he used to row on the river.

Two in the morning they had left. Josie remembered feeling tipsy; she had consumed a large amount of wine, something that she was not accustomed to doing, and when Richard had stood up and said, "Come on, it's time you were in bed," panic had nearly set in. Her muddled mind tried to work out, was it his bed? Her bed? These thoughts passed in a flash, as it took all her concentration to stand up and walk to the door. There had been an anti-climax on the first date; the same taxi was waiting outside for them and in no time at all it reached her house, though she had not given her escort the address. Opening the door and halting her stumble, he had kissed her lightly on the cheek: "I'll call you tomorrow at the hospital."

Yes, she had mumbled, fumbling for her key. She could have swore it was only seconds, but on looking up cab and Richard had disappeared. They had gone out together over the next couple of weeks, always the same transport, and not once had she glimpsed the driver. Richard and she had grown slowly together, but not once had he put a foot inside her door. Although his kisses on leaving were of a passionate nature they came short and sharp as if he wanted to move on, then one day he had said, so casual, "Joe, I would like you to move in with me." This came as a shock as she had not an inkling of where he lived in London. What about her life? It would be turned upside down—the house, should she rent it or sell? It was close to the hospital, so there would be no problems doing either. Grinning broadly, he waited for her answer, and as she had found in the many instances then and since, he was always two steps ahead of her. The house? All taken care off, sell or rent, just phone this number they will take care of it, whatever you decide, also the moving of any furniture you may want to bring.

She remembered protesting feebly, bastard Richard, you have walked into my life, now you want to turn it upside down. She laughed inwardly as she remembered thumping his arm as he grinned wickedly and came back with his reply: "But that is what you want, Joe."

They squeezed hands tightly across the table and it was sealed. The waiter broke their concentration; Josie ordered chocolate ice-cream for dessert, while Richard declined. He just sat back waiting for her next move. "Richard," she had smiled sweetly, "can I see your flat before I move in?"

"Sorry, no can do," he had replied. "I will be away for at least three weeks. When I get back, be there, Joe."

Other people in the restaurant looked across as she protested loudly, but he just sat back and watched her with a faint smile on his face. That evening as usual their transport was waiting, but this time it drew up outside a smart hotel. She remembered following Richard closely without looking left or right as they walked across to the lift.

Both their emotions erupted that night, taking her into heights that she had never experienced before, and leaving her completely exhausted.

Then waking in the morning to find her lover gone, panic had gripped her again until she saw the neat writing on the hotel stationary.

"I love you, Joe," and kisses were scrawled across the page. "Bill is paid, enjoy your breakfast, see you in a few weeks, my address and your contact telephone number will be delivered to you at the hospital. Love Richard."

"Penny for your thoughts, Josie?" Catherine was

looking at her questioningly. "Cup of tea? You look like you could do with one."

Josie tried to stop herself looking at the stairs where moments before, or was it minutes, Richard had disappeared, and concentrate on the present.

"Yes please, two sugars, no, you had better make that just one." Then she smiled to herself, because really, three would have been better.

"Come on then, let's go into the kitchen. Now I'm going to gain another daughter, we should get to know each other."

Josie did not waver from the truth that they had lived together, but she did not tell Catherine the whole story of his proposal to her.

Richard had come in on evening and said so matter-of-factly, "Joe, let's get married?

The answer from her was, "Yes of course, love, when?"

The Barbados wedding was a *fait-accompli*; it had all been arranged; the only thing he had asked her opinion about, was did she think it was a good idea if they asked his family to fly out with them? When her answer was in the affirmative, he had casually taken the flight tickets from his coat jacket.

Catherine laughed when she told her of her weakness for chocolates, how in the ward the patients would offer sweet temptations her way, how she had tried to go on a diet, which only lasted part of a day. Richard had sat in front of her with an open box, asking her opinion on their taste, then he had teased her until she had joined him, munching joyfully.

Catherine replied in kind; how she had always worried over her son, how in the early years they had seen him fairly often, but how, for the last couple, they had hardly seen him at all, and how it had come as a great shock to the family that he had been wounded.

Josie listened intently. Richard had said that his father was something to do with banking and would be away from home more than he was. This was not true, only a few times a year would he be away for any length of time; at the moment he was in Manchester, but would be joining them as soon as possible. Josie told Catherine how her son had a scrapbook pasted with his sister's achievements over the years, and how proud he was for her that she had been selected to ride in the big event. How she was completely fearless on Kelly her horse, and how with their combined skills it had pushed them to the point of riding against the best in the world.

"Hope you and Richard are coming? It's only a few miles away from here."

"Yes, I believe we are, now you come to mention it, Friday lunch-time."

Josie sipped her tea pondering; the girl upstairs must be something special. Even with Josie's scant knowledge of horses, she realised that to be selected to ride in the company of Olympic team members must be daunting to say the least.

Katrina heard her brother mount the stairs, the wood creaking under his weight, then the slight pause as he reached her bedroom door. She held her breath, then he passed by. Feeling guilty and embarrassed at having rushed past her mother and the bride-to-be as they waited for her by the gate, she tried to calm down.

Reaching out from the bed where she lay, she opened the door of the wardrobe. Katrina looked at her reflection in the mirror; only a slight puffiness around the eyes betrayed the flood-gates that had opened. From the half-opened window she could hear the chatter from the kitchen as lunch was being prepared. Pushing herself off the bed, she moved to the small white unit tucked away in the corner of her room. Opening a drawer, she looked for the small object wrapped in tissue paper, then clutching it tightly she made quickly for the top of the stairs. Slowly she descended, each foot placed outward to try and prevent any betrayal of her passage, and so intent was she on not making a noise, that she completely failed to see her mother staring up at her.

"Katrina, what the earth are you doing?"

Nearly falling the last three steps with fright, she tried to compose herself and find some excuse for creeping down the stairs. Josie had joined her mother, so completely ignoring the question, she held out her hand to her.

"Congratulations, I am sorry for earlier."

"That's all right, your brother does have the same effect on me sometimes." They both laughed.

Gathering her car keys from the rack, and walking towards the front door in haste, she called out, "Going to see Kelly."

"Katrina, don't be long, lunch will be ready in half an hour, Joe and Richard are starving."

She noticed that already her mother had dropped the end of Josie's name. That was good, because if her brother loved her so should all the family.

Backing the MG soft-top out of the drive, she tried to analyse the plan that had formulated in her mind.

James clawed his way up the steep grassy bank close to the trees and bushes. It was hard-going, the slope was at least forty-five degrees and it did not help that the sole of his shoes had no grip. The watcher looked on in anger: what had his son said to the girl to make her suddenly run away? Anything untoward could affect the relationship built up over a number of years with the local landowners. James made the flat ground with one final effort, then collapsed and tore at his tie, great gasps came from him as he fought for air.

John walked over. "What the hell are you playing at, boy, why did that girl run away? What did you say to upset her?"

Still panting he looked up at the thunderous face staring down at him, "Dad, you've got it all wrong." Then he stood up and gave a ritual dance with his metal detector. "That was her brother calling, didn't you hear? That's why she ran, so there."

John calmed down immediately. "From where I was looking it seemed as if you'd scared her."

"No way, I'm going to meet her again, what do you

say about that then?—and her name is Katrina."

"Is it now? You will have to get fit pretty quick, what if she asks you to go riding with her, tell her you don't know how?"

"Dad, is it time to go?"

"No it's not, you were asleep for an hour, scrambled down the bank, nearly gave me a heart attack with the rider! No, we are not going just now just so you can go in the pub early, It's eleven-forty-five, we will go at twelve-thirty."

"This path runs along the side of the field to the road. I am not going back the way we came, so I will see you later. Okay."

There was no intention in his mind of sticking to the path, and when he had skirted the copse he angled down towards the houses that he could see through the trees. All his instincts pushed him forward while something in the back of his mind said he was a fool.

James faltered now he was at the exit from the valley, and now, as he stood close to the gate, all of his bravado with his father seemed to have melted away. He knew it would take a lot of his courage to step out into the open. What if Katrina was watching? She would know at once that he had been tracking her down.

What the hell! He was twenty-three years old, a partner in his father's printing firm, drove a Ford Escort TRI, the latest model. Now he was skulking around in the bushes like a fourteen-year-old school boy waiting to carry books for his first crush.

From his bedroom window Richard saw the slight movement under the trees near the entrance to the valley, so he rummaged in a drawer and brought out a pair of high-powered binoculars. Moving back into the room so that there would be no chance that the sun glinting on the glass would betray his presence, he focused in on the still figure. Twenty-five, maybe a couple of years younger, it was hard to tell with those streaks of green running down his face like camouflage, six foot at least—he was furtively looking up and down the road. Richard pursed his lips and grinned; he knew at once what ailed his sister—this must be her new boyfriend, or from her actions this morning, maybe her lover?

"My, my," he spoke out loud, "I wonder what has happened to Rodrick." Only a few minutes ago the throaty roar of his sister's car had brought him to the window, and he had watched Katrina drive down the road and over the bridge. Unbeknown to James, she had skirted the valley on the other side, and was making her way back to Home Farm by an alternative route. Richard still watched. It puzzled him that the young man did not look directly at their house once but seemed to be scanning the whole village. Now he was in the middle of the black tarmac road, completely in the open. He paused for a few seconds, shook his head, then trudged up the slope till he was lost from sight. There was no doubt in his mind, that his sister had never brought whoever he was to their home, so this must be a secret liaison. Then he frowned, what the hell, Katrina was a woman and nature would take its course. "I wonder if Father knows, better for her that he doesn't."

Looking across the rolling hills he vividly remembered when it was his turn to go through the pangs of first love—a farmer's daughter not far away in the next village—and the problems it had caused with his father. This had soured his relationship within the family, and when he was successful in getting a place at Oxford University he could not wait to get away.

Learning came naturally and there were plenty of sporting activities to pursue. He had progressed and passed out with honours; the coveted rowing blue was his too with the distinction of winning against Cambridge two years in succession. There was also the freedom of going out with any female of his choice, so when George had mentioned joining his firm he had declined, office work was not for him to knuckle down to.

Much to his father's displeasure, and despite his mother's pleading, he had taken a commission in the army. From the beginning it seemed that he had chosen well: there were many visits home but, as he progressed into other dimensions, they had become less frequent. He found the change from acute danger back to the slowness of rural life unreal and unsettling—one part of his mind longed for peace and quiet, while the other would not accept the change. Catherine and George now gave all their love and affection to Katrina, which was only right, and material things were heaped on her too. Kelly, her eventing and show-jumping horse, cost over four thousand pounds four years ago, and now he was eight and a half years old and worth a hell of a lot more. That had been her sixteenth birthday present. Now the sports car, a few weeks ago, for her twentieth. It would come as a big shock to find suddenly that their daughter had grown into a woman, and was seeing a young man without their knowledge. Then he laughed. Why am I worrying? With Joe to love, in the future we may be able to provide a few grandchildren for them, god willing! Then he banged the door and went down the stairs. "Mother, lunch ready?"

George had left the suburbs of Manchester and was trying to tune in to the latest traffic information as his large BMW purred contentedly, swishing its driver towards home. He had been annoyed temporarily when the secretary had interrupted his meeting with the area managers. "Telephone call, Mr Chambers, from your wife."

Taking the call outside the boardroom, he had listened intently as Catherine, highly excited, told him the good news, then he walked in and asked, "Any of you gentlemen been to Barbados?" One member of the group put up a weak hand.

"I have, sir."

"Well, come on then, tell us all about the place."

Nervously at first, but more fluently as he saw that no one was going to interrupt and that they were all listening, he spoke of the hospitality of the place, how clear was the sea, of the smell of the flowers, of night clubs and the limbo dancers.

George interrupted. "Were you married there?"

"Um, no, sir."

"Well my son is going to be."

They looked blankly at this statement.

"In two week's time—the family are going too, so that means me. That should make you happy. Come on then, let's get this meeting over."

One hour later Gene Pitney came through loud and clear from the radio, and the driver tapped one foot to the music as the motorway rapidly decreased the distance between him and his family.

Katrina drove into the empty stable yard. She had prayed that Alan was still in the vicinity, and her wish had been granted as a puff of smoke and the noise of a tractor came from the adjacent field. Climbing the gate and sprinting until it came into sight, she slowed and walked purposely towards the machine that enclosed the driver in its cab. Seeing her frantically waving, he cut the noise from the engine and climbed down to greet her. "Everything all right?"

Katrina bit her lip before replying, "Well, yes, do you think the detectors would be interested in looking at this coin I found?" Katrina unwrapped the thick unblemished Roman bronze, and standing proud of the surface stood the small figures of Romulus and Remus with their mother the She Wolf.

"Very nice, shall I keep it for you and show it to them when they next come up, or shall I phone John? He may come up in the week if you wish. Where did you find it?" Katrina pointed towards the village but did not say exactly where the coin was found.

Alan looked at her and smiled. "Maybe if John can't come, Tony might."

"James," she replied, and she knew that when the word left her lips it was a mistake.

Alan looked through narrowed eyes as the girl blushed a bright pink. He knew something had been troubling her over the last few weeks but he had mistakenly put it down to the forthcoming riding event. Looking away from her he gave the rider time to compose herself. "Have you seen them this morning?"

Straight back came the reply, "In the valley, both of them, earlier."

"I'll tell you what, when I get back to the house I'll phone you with their number so you can contact them yourself. Okay? Say around one o'clock, that suit you?"

"That's fine, thank you, I will not be going out this afternoon."

Katrina turned away, then stopped. "By the way, Alan, Richard is home and he's getting married in two weeks' time."

"Good luck to him," came back faintly on the wind as the chimney stack shook and a puff of smoke spiralled upwards to break the clean air.

Katrina walked in the open front door. Richard was

snuggled close to Josie with his head on her shoulders and his hands clasped around her waist. He looked quizzically at his sister but did not speak. This knowing gaze almost unnerved her but she ignored his stare and flounced into the kitchen. Catherine called, "Five minutes or we'll sit down without you. When are you going to get changed? You've had those clothes on all morning."

She felt herself stiffen at these words. "Mother, don't fuss, you do carry on. I'll have a bath now, if you don't mind."

"I don't mind at all, if you want to smell that's your problem."

The last remark took her by surprise, but it was true: any work-out with the horse always left her wringing wet all over. Usually it was straight home, quickly into the bath or shower with plenty of soap and foam to wash away the perspiration, but today her thoughts were on more important things. How would her mother understand even if she told her?

Richard hugged Josie more tightly and mouthed a few words in her ear, undetected by the two antagonists.

"A young man, you have seen him?"

He nodded. "That's why she is so skittish."

Catherine was not happy; there definitely was something amiss, but for the moment it completely eluded her.

3

John rapped the window of the parked vehicle, for James was slumped in his favourite position with eyelids closed as though asleep. Except he was only pretending, because pretty pictures drifted across his vision much clearer with closed eyes than with them open. Leaning across he opened the catch so that his father could get in the driving seat.

"Did you find anything good?" he asked.

"No, only the usual rubbish, a few pieces of bronze and an old battered brooch. What about yourself? As if I don't know—it looks as if you have had a better morning than me."

"Lay off, Dad, I don't even know her."

"But you will, my boy, I bet you will, wait till I tell your mother."

"Look, just drop it. It's bad enough when she complains when I come in late, without giving her any other excuse to harangue me." James looked glumly out of the car, not looking forward to going home at all. There would be questions, he knew, but no answers that would make any sense.

They pulled up at the junction of the main Bath to Stroud road, turned right and crossed the motorway, then turned left and drifted down the sharp bends towards their destination. Neither had spoken for the first few miles they had travelled, then the passenger broke the silence. "Are you going shopping this afternoon?"

"Probably, why?"

James did not answer for a few seconds, although his thoughts were fully focused on his answer.

"Well?" He paused again.

"Can I borrow your metal detector for a couple of hours? It's not so hard on the ears as mine."

The driver looked in the rear view mirror, saw that the road was devoid of any following traffic, slowed the car, then burst out laughing. "You are going, how can I put it, wooing, with a coin searcher, not a bunch of flowers?" John raised his voice to emphasise the next sentence. "Do you know who the hell that young lady is?" Then more quietly, almost in awe, "Her surname is Chambers, and the family own acres and acres of land including the valley where we were this morning. But best of all, next Thursday, Badminton… ." He gave a slight nudge with his elbow. "Horses going over large fences, only the best invited to compete, and guess what, who is going to ride at this prestigious meeting?"

James held his silence, as his father carefully negotiated the gap between the two iron gates at the entrance to the drive of their bungalow. Just as the dog started to bark a greeting the phone rang. Betty picked it up; a male voice answered, "Is James there please?"

Whoever it was said please, usually it was just a grunt, then James or Jammer, his nickname. "Who is it?"

There was hesitation on the line.

"Would you give him a message? Just ask him to phone this number, it could be to his advantage."

Betty scribbled the number down as the two of them walked in the door. Talking into the mouthpiece she said, "He is here, I'll get him to speak to you."

James took the receiver but whoever it was had rung off. The note was passed to him by his mother who saw fully for the first time his attire. "My God, you look like a scarecrow."

Before he could be berated any more, he turned and walked into the bathroom and locked the door. Muffled tones reached him as his father took the full brunt of attack, then suddenly it went very quiet and he knew that his secret was out.

"James." His mother was speaking in a more considerate tone. "The water is all right for a bath."

Grinning, he swished the suds on top of the water so that it foamed like the froth on a pint of beer, and looking at his watch he saw that he was late already. His mates would already be on their second glass and would be wondering if he was going to the match this afternoon. Making a mental note, five minutes in the bath, four minutes to get dressed and three to run to the local, if he could run, just enough time for a quick one—that would be his lot. The telephone number floated to the floor as he dressed quickly, hurriedly picking it up he scrutinised the number closely.

"Mother, that phone call, who was it?"

Betty shrugged her shoulders.

"Whoever it was did not give a name, only left this number."

"Right I'm off for a quick pint, then the match, see you later."

John broke in on their conversation: "Why don't you phone, and see who it is?"

"But I have no time."

"What you mean is you won't have time for a drink, eh boy?"

"Okay, come on then." James picked up the object that was holding him back from his colleagues, burr, burr.

Catherine picked the receiver up. A young male voice came through: "I have been asked to call, my name is James." It was not for her.

"Richard, someone on the phone—he's been asked to call our number, his name is James, is it for you?"

Josie looked at Richard, who looked wickedly at Katrina, while Catherine gazed at all of them.

Katrina stood up: "It's for me, Mother."

She walked across the room unsteadily. All the strength seemed to have gone from her legs. Alan had set her up, it was so obvious. The back of her knuckles showed white with her grip and she whispered, "Hello."

"This is James."

Then he knew who it was.

"Is that Katrina?"

"Yes." The musical voice answered in a whisper.

"Christ!" James dropped the telephone with a clatter onto the table.

She heard him swear and the sound as the receiver hit some object. Katrina was now completely in control of her nerves, although she wondered if her heartbeat could be heard in the room. James was trying to work out how he could see her soon, and while he was thinking of a solution, his connection was telling him of Alan's intervention with the coin that she had shown him.

"Katrina are you going anywhere this afternoon?" but before her answer came down the line, more words tumbled out: "I could meet you at the stable where you keep your horse, around two o'clock, is that okay?"

"Yes, that is fine, James, I'll see you soon, bye."

Reluctantly the receiver was replaced for she wanted to say so much. Why, if only there was a phone in her bedroom, or the mobile one that she had asked for so many times in the past. This would have to be a top priority, it was ridiculous, even sixteen-year-olds, and some even younger could talk in private. There she was, twenty, frustrated, angry, and trying to communicate her innermost thoughts within hearing distance of a room full of people.

Turning away from the now dead line, she looked across at Richard and Josie who were trying hard not to laugh, both had their hands over mouths that were bursting with mirth.

Catherine spoke with an icy edge to her voice, "Who was that?"

"No one, Mother, just a friend," she answered, fully in control of the situation. "Josie, I'm sorry but I won't be able to help you unpack, I'm going out."

"That's all right, we understand, don't we, Richard?"

Katrina flounced out of the room just as they both burst out laughing. Catherine knew for sure there was something going on and she must get in on the secret quickly, at least before George arrived home.

"Come on, tell me what is going on?"

"Mother, don't you know?"

"Well, is it that Katrina is worried about the flight, or Kelly, and who was that on the phone?"

"You're way off the truth, the person on the phone is her new man friend and our kiddo is completely besotted with him."

"Richard, what do you mean? Rodrick is her—" Catherine paused aghast as she realised that only this afternoon he would arrive with a proposal and a ring to match.

Josie piped up, "She is in love, Mrs Chambers, totally and completely."

Catherine put her hand over her mouth more in shook than anger. But what about Rodrick she thought, my secret, they were going to get engaged this afternoon, he told me only a few days ago.

More complications to deal with thought Catherine

before continuing, "Charles will be furious, I really don't know what he's going to say."

Katrina gathered a wool cardigan from the wardrobe, although the temperature hovered around the sixty degree mark for there was no knowing what time she would return home. She smiled wickedly—if at all! At least the covering would keep her warm if it was needed. Looking at her watch she felt slightly nervous, not of the possibility that he would not turn up, but of knowing that whatever he desired of her she would give willingly without any reservation.

She felt the surge in her body again, and the feeling increased while looking at her reflection in the mirror. Hair swept back and plaited into one long pony-tail, a heavy triple-strand interwoven gold necklace encircled a slim neck. The white crop-top emphasised her taut breasts, and her nipples were proud and plainly visible. A brown bare midriff showed above a slim buckled belt holding tight stretch trousers that enclosed shapely thighs and tapered down her legs to plain flat shoes.

What to wear had been a problem: her physical outward feelings for her love dared her to wear her one and only mini skirt. This hugged her like a glove and with long legs would set the brief piece of material off perfectly, but she had given in to her inner warning thoughts and discarded what had been the first choice. Katrina looked in the full-length mirror: critical was the gaze, every and each part of the reflected face was scanned for flaws. They were there—the most prominent ran from her right eyebrow to disappear into the hairline, a jagged white scar. Now the spring sun and wind tanning her countenance seemed to magnify the ugly mark out of all proportion. Expertly the camouflage from the make-up box was applied until she was satisfied that the disfigurement had completely disappeared. Looking at the watch for the fourth time in as many minutes, Katrina felt slightly apprehensive—yes, her nose was much too large. What if he liked small ones, turned up on the end, not straight and fat like hers?

"Katrina!" The sound came from downstairs, then grew louder: "Katy, Rodrick's on the phone."

Although it was early, all her senses said go now. From the bedroom and down the stairs lightly she tiptoed so that if the person on the other end of the line was listening he would not hear her passage. Catherine was holding her hand across the mouthpiece: "Are you going riding with him later?" The words came out almost pleadingly, and as they were spoken Katrina noticed that her mother was nodding her head up and down as if to influence her decision.

"Not today, Mother, I'm going out."

Catherine, looking at her daughter, was almost startled—the clothes were not for riding that was for sure; you could even see the outline of her briefs, and it was an effort not to look at her bare midriff. Where had they come from? Most of the time they shopped together, and these were not her style at all.

"Later then, what time shall I say?"

"No, no, no, tell him I'm ill, or anything you want, I must go."

There was no sign of Richard or Josie, and as her mother talked to Rodrick (trying not to lie but at the same time giving excuses for her non-attendance), Katrina silently opened the front door and ran to her car parked in the drive.

Four minutes later the cattle grid sounded a protest as the weight of the vehicle rattled across its metal struts. Slowly she drove down the slope before accelerating up the steep drive into the stable yard. Katrina sat for a moment; all was at peace—it was not like the early-morning chaos, especially on a Saturday like today. Kelly snorted a greeting, then twitched his ears as always, as if to say come on, then let's go, but she patted his head, then gently whispered why today he would take second place in her affections.

Bang, bang, away behind her, at least the marksman was not in the valley. Then she saw him coming: all her anger was dissipated to be replaced by a feeling of expectation, wicked green light shone from narrowed eyelids as she squinted against the bright sun angling across the trees. Her body was leaning against a dry stone wall that acted as a support. Although outwardly trying to give the impression of calm, her insides felt just like jelly. Slowly the car came into the yard; the driver slightly turned his head, nodded once at her beckon, then parked where she indicated. The door opened, and from the interior he emerged slowly, then he stood up, and with quick strides came towards where she was standing. Outstretched arms reached out eagerly for him and their fingers locked together. Katrina tried to release her foot from the wall to pull him in closer to her body, but her bent knee interrupted his progress, so he leaned forward and kissed her lightly on the cheek. Gripping his hands tightly, she turned her mouth to his, how sweet was her moment of fulfilment as he responded, oblivious to anyone watching. Time was only for each other, whether in a dusty street, a subway, this was their very first kiss, so where it took place was not important, only the fact that it had. Katrina pushed herself forward, gripping her love more tightly, so that her foot could be released from the wall.

"Katrina," he gasped, and then felt her body sway.

"Pins and needles," she whispered.

James laughed out loud as his large hands encircled her waist to give her body some support. The skin of her bare midriff felt like velvet and his strength seemed to multiply so that her whole frame felt as light as a feather, even completely suspended from the ground. Goose pimples multiplied across her back as his fingers slide across her hot bare skin, then her nipples hardened as they moved forward to cup her whole breasts. His eyes were closed as his mouth worked with hers, and his frame felt hard like a coiled spring. Katrina already wanted him to merge now as one, and in these brief moments every part of her was completely anaesthetised. Never in her life had she experienced feelings of this magnitude.

"Hey! Have you permission?"

The words were spoken in a Southern American accent, soft and drawn out, without even a hint of intimidation. James felt the skin on his knuckles scrape against the wall as he turned in fright at this intrusion, his exploring had taken him much lower and his palms were cupping two round mounds so that their lower regions would fuse together as his hands tightened. The girl trainee from South Carolina gasped, as a red-faced dishevelled fellow rider emerged from the other side of the standing stranger.

"Katy, I never saw you, I thought that—" the girl paused "—you know, he was doing something against the wall." The double meaning in her words and the expression on her smiling face warned both of them that probably Mary Joe had watched them from the first instant of their meeting.

"Spying on me, you minx," Katrina moved forward. "When I catch you—" The last few words were not spoken as a door opened in the farmhouse, and a more than ample woman gave harassed sign language across the stable yard. James could make out "phone" for sure as his love moved quickly to join her. They both seemed agitated as if cross words were being banded between them. Katrina shook her head violently, and he could swear that she stamped her foot in protest. Whatever had been said its impact had devastated her euphoric countenance. Now a deep frown replaced the radiance of a few minutes before and for the first time he saw the white miniature tree-like scar on her forehead. James waited, not saying a word as Katrina moved slowly closer in deep thought. When his arms encircled her waist it was almost as though he was supporting a floppy rag doll. Just a few minutes ago he was trying to hold down five feet-eight inches of sexual dynamite, now someone or something had extinguished that fire and at the same time lopped more than a few inches off her height, for her frame had shrunk dramatically. Clinging to him, the smell and warmth of his body gave her strength so that within a short time their heartbeats became one. Looking up into his eyes, Katrina saw the quizzical question mark written in his gaze but this was not the time or place to give him the answer. They must leave now as quickly as possible. Then he gently kissed her forehead, and she shuddered as his moist lips felt full of softness and caring, not passion. One fierce hug to show her tremendous appreciation of his gesture, then she pulled away and turned towards the young American girl who was hopping about on one foot.

"If you want stay part of my team at Badminton, you will do exactly as I say." The tone of the voice was almost a command; no one had ever asked Mary Joe to help with a horse of near Olympic standard, and whatever the rider asked she would do willingly.

"Yes, Katrina," came the meek reply.

James watched in amazement as a torrent of words were directed at the attentive listener, who seemed to nod in the right places. As for himself, most of the jargon was alien to his ears. Glancing at his watch the hands showed two-twenty. He knew that they had met a few minutes earlier, but so much had gone on in the last half an hour that it was making his head spin.

"Come on, we must hurry."

James was hoping that they might walk or preferably run and hide themselves away in the valley, so that their brief aborted passion could be rekindled. Besides, there were a few questions ascertaining to her animated conversation not many minutes before that needed at least some explaining. His dream—of a gentle stroll across the grass meadow and beyond, then to lie in the shade beside her with no one to intrude—looked doomed, for Katrina opened the door of her MG, slipped inside, then urgently beckoned him to join her. The seat belt seemed twisted in its housing, and only came reluctantly as he tried to lock the buckle in place, but before his task was completed the spitfire car was blasting along the narrow lanes.

Click, at last, he looked up at the face of the driver and noticed the bottom edges of her white teeth protruding over the lower lip. Tension around her mouth betrayed her inner thoughts but the hands on the steering wheel seemed light and responsive to the needs of the speed. Sixty, forty, he felt himself going forward against the restraints as deceleration took place rapidly, then the car stopped in a shower of gravel. Katrina switched off the engine before slumping back in the driver's leather seat. Almost at once in the rear view mirror a car appeared in the distance. Tense, she held her breath; only when the motor had passed without the occupants even giving a glance towards them could she relax in part.

James watched her facial expressions keenly; her head was still slightly tilted and he knew that the road behind was still being scanned. Doubts began to manifest in his thoughts: they had hardly talked since they had met. Who was his love running away from, her fiancé, father? This was the time to find out.

"Penny for your thoughts, James."

He opened his eyes wide with a start, his mind always worked better with them half-closed or so he always told anyone who caught him analysing a problem and who ventured to ask. Katrina was looking at him with a broad smile on her face. Gone was the tenseness from around her mouth, nor was there any other sign of tension. It was as if someone had opened the door and let the sunlight in.

Rose had given her a fright in the stable yard. Rodrick had telephoned the farm to ask if she was there, and had been told that she was. As luck would have it she had received the message before he had arrived and bolted. There was no going back: James would be her lover in every sense before the day was over, and she shuddered thinking about the pleasure that had never been hers, as she started to plan for this final fulfilment. "James—" There was no need to call his name, all his avid attention was focused on her, and he waited for her to continue.

"Where would you have gone this afternoon, if you were not with me?"

"That's easy, two pints of lager at my local with my mates, then have a lift to see the last home game of the season." Then he laughed. "It's comical, I completely forgot that it was my turn to drive, I wonder if they are still waiting?" Then he added lightly, "You see what effect your spell-binding beauty is having on me."

Katrina blushed, and leaned across to ruffle his dark hair. Only a few minutes ago her intention was to drive out of the local area quickly, maybe across to Bristol if her love so wished, then, later, return to her valley. Another idea that was already formulating was that the safest place would be amongst a crowd. Rodrick would not even think that she had gone to a football match, or anyone at the stables either. Anyway, why was she worried? The decision to drive where she wanted and with the person she adored, was hers and hers alone, not her mother and father's, or anyone else.

"James would you believe that I have never been to a game?" The tone was soft with just a hint of expectation in its delivery. Only an hour or two ago the answer would have been easy. But at this moment, at twenty-five minutes to three on a sunny May afternoon while parked in a dusty lay-by, his thoughts were more in tune with the idea of physical contact between just the two of them than with sharing a part of her with strangers, even if it was only a glance or passing comment. With narrowed eyelids, he was watching her, and on his forehead little beads of perspiration began to show. Katrina knew exactly what he was thinking but this was not the time or place.

"Three o'clock they kick off." The tone was of resignation, then brightened up considerably as he went on speaking. "I usually find a space near the park, then it's only a few minutes' walk to the ground—the way you drive we should make the start easily." All he received for his information and observation was the tip of a pink tongue, as the engine roared into life, and they moved off at a stately ten miles an hour.

Rodrick was not happy, of Katy there was no sign, and Rose could not help him although she swore that his message had been passed on. Mary Joe, whom he detested because of her accent, was fussing with Kelly much to his astonishment, since Katrina never let anyone go near her horse except the stable owner. Her answer to his question hurt the more, because she described in graphic detail the young man Katy had driven off with, telling him that she had agreed to bed down the horse later as they would not return until at least dusk. This was ridiculous: they had always been together since their early teens, except for a short time when he had let the branch go that had almost scalped her. Of course it had been an accident, everyone said so—Katy should have been wearing a hard hat. Then he scowled as he remembered that her brother was not so forgiving. Maybe someone from Badminton, a member of the committee, had called in to see her? Rodrick brightened up at this thought, but as his large Range Rover slowly passed the sporty Ford Escort he was not so sure.

The driver was frustrated as he inched slowly forward in the thick traffic. Did they not know that he was one of the football coaches, with only six minutes remaining to the kick-off? How many goalkeepers had been taken to hospital in the last few weeks?—three at least, counting the one who had been injured this morning, and even now the first-choice keeper was playing with an injured wrist. The season had been extended by two weeks due to the number of cancelled matches over the winter period, but now the hard sun-baked grounds were extracting a heavy toll from the players. Still four games to play, not including today's! Slowly the car moved forward a few more yards, then stopped. His gaze wandered towards a young couple walking with the flow of people on the other side of the road. Then he saw the grinning face of James Eagles, and, swinging out of the line of traffic, he drove across the road to intercept the pair, scattering more than a few pedestrians who had decided to brave the traffic at this point. Tony expertly parked the Mitsubishi Shogun just in front of his quarry, then leaned out of the open window. There were no need for introductions as they both knew each other well.

"I need a big favour, James—look I'm late already, why don't you and um—" he nodded at Katrina, "—be my guest for the match today."

James weighed the remark up quickly: "Okay, Tony, let's go."

Although the stadium was only a few streets away, it was still a white-knuckle ride as the driver tried to make up time. Tony drove into his private parking space with a squeal of brakes, and almost before the Shogun was stationary he had opened their door. "Come on you two, hurry, they're starting."

Urgently he ushered them into the ground, and they both watched in silence as he spoke a few words to an official, at the same time pointing towards the stand and themselves. Quickly their benefactor came over to where they stood. "James, wait for me after the game, don't disappear. Oh! Pleased to meet you, young lady." Then he was gone.

The players were already out on the pitch with only a minute to go before the start of play, when the two of them were taken to their seats in the stand. They had been given seats in a place always reserved for dignitaries or possible new team members. James looked around proudly; if he had not met Katrina today he would just have been a face in the crowd of supporters on the terracing. This beautiful girl was holding his hand tightly as the excitement mounted around them; it made his nerves tingle with anticipation for his love, and also for the game.

Local television cameras scanned the ground looking for any interesting possibilities amongst the maze of faces, when the lens finally focused on the couple sitting in the seats reserved for possible new signings.

James wondered what Tony wanted and guessed correctly that he needed another keeper. To his horror he remembered puffing up the slope in the morning—was it only a few hours ago? Looking at her unashamedly and with adoration in his eyes he knew that all his efforts had been more than repaid in full.

"Katrina, are you sure that you haven't been to a match before?"

"No, never. James—" she entwined her arm around his and pulled him close, "—which team is ours?"

He kissed her lightly on the lips, and pointed.

The home team played well and Katrina soon became absorbed in the action as the highs and lows on the pitch were transmitted to the crowd. When they came in at half-time they were winning—two goals to nil. The steward primed to look after the couple ushered them into a lounge type bar: "Help yourselves, sandwiches, coffee, tea, all free."

The bar was open, and that interested James more, but he looked at Katrina and put all thoughts of a pint from his mind.

Across the pitch his mates were looking for him in the crowd; it was unusual that he had not turned up. Someone had borrowed a small pair of binoculars, and, noticing that one of the cameras was pointed in the direction of the stand, focused in. "Look, there he is."

"Where?"

"Look, over there in the stand, with that girl."

"Bloody hell, who's he with the manager's daughter, no wonder he dumped us."

They were all looking across now, and the unfortunate stand-in driver of their transport felt really peeved. "He will have to bloody well walk home. Did you notice that he never came up the pub? Didn't buy me a pint, selfish sod. Ya, he can bloody well walk."

They all laughed at his remarks, and pushed him. "She's better looking than you, Nobby," one chided.

Another, more brave, said, "Come to think of it, you're real ugly."

Then the teams came out to restart the game, and their pal and his female companion were forgotten for the moment as the ball was worked swiftly and dangerously into the opposing team's penalty area. There was plenty of cheering and arm-waving throughout the second half, and when Katrina jumped up in excitement even more of her bare midriff was exposed than if she had sat meekly in her seat. Both were flushed at the end of the game, although the score remained two-nil to their team. There had been moments when Katrina had just put her arms around him, closed her eyes and hoped that their opponents did not put the ball in the net. James was elated: sat close up against his body was someone that he had waited for, the girl of his dreams, and he knew that by her flushed face and sparkling eyes the afternoon was a complete success.

Tony came straight to the point. "I need a keeper, you available?"

James nodded.

"How fit are you?"

He shrugged his shoulders.

"Okay, you know the score, I only train the best, tomorrow morning, nine-thirty if you are up to it, any problem with transport?"

James shook his head while Katrina hovered a few yards away.

Tony watched as the two of them walked away hand in hand—funny chap, he hardly ever joined in any pre-match banter, a real loner. Even if he had played brilliantly, his team-mates were never sure how to congratulate him, and there was always that hint of tension in the dressing room. Some of the players had made the sly comment that what he needed was a good woman—well, maybe that had happened? Tony felt more upbeat as he turned away from the retreating figures; they had won the game, and he had found a true professional to join the squad for the rest of the short season.

They were now outside the ground, and just a few stragglers were still leaving. James noticed that the sun was already close to the roof-tops, and, as they walked together, a light breeze blew discarded paper along the gutters. They had entered the park before James could bring himself to ask her an important question.

"Katrina, what time do you have to be home?"

"There is no time limit, silly. Although if we are staying out to the early hours of the morning, Mother will expect me to call and let her know." She let go of his hand: "Unless you want me to go now?"

"No way, come here."

Then as he moved forward, she laughed, calling, "Catch me if you can."

Sometimes he would win and force a laughing kiss as his reward, or she would slip away easily, unchecked, but every time they touched, their temperatures seemed to rise dramatically.

"Your chariot awaits you," she teased as they reached her car. "Whither will it take us? Yours is my command." Then, modifying her tone slightly, "What do you want to do?"

Katrina judged his mood quite perfectly and pulled him in tight to her body. Then he felt a tremendous heat as if they were both on fire. Face on, their eyes locked on each other's so that they seemed to blur into one.

Huskily she whispered, "Do you love me?"

"Yes," he replied, hardly getting the words out as their lips sought each other.

"Mummy, Mummy, what are those two people doing?" a small squeaky voice piped. Reluctantly they parted as the tiny tot looked up at the two of them with wide staring eyes.

Both their faces were flushed, and with passion still running high they quickly sought the enclosed sanctuary of the car. Only when they were safely inside did they burst out laughing, for the small child, now firmly held by the hand, was trying to peer in the window as she was dragged away.

Katrina felt a strange sensation, one that she had not experienced ever, as within this cocoon she could feel the electricity and the tension magnified between them. It seemed that as the hours moved slowly towards dusk, their awareness of each other's need was heightened. Neither of them spoke as each with their own thoughts waited for the other.

James watched as her fingers played idly with the key that was ready to power the engine into life and transport them to wherever they desired.

"Toll bridge the other side of the town, I believe it's called Bathampton; we could go for a walk along the canal if you like?"

The words came out in a rush as the idea came to him. This was the only place he knew within the Bath area, as a few years ago he had gone fishing for pike near the weir. Besides, and as far as he could remember for certain, close by was an excellent place for a meal and a pint or two.

The green dart sped around the outskirts of the city, and his eyes were only for her as he watched the pedals move up and down smoothly under her touch as she drove. Seated so close to her, he was fascinated by the rise and fall of her taut breasts, and his hand moved across unconsciously to feel her bare hot skin above the buckled belt. As he did so, he felt a shiver run through her body. Then his hand, as if it had a mind of its own, moved slowly and secretly upwards, until its fingers were out of sight, climbed until it completely enclosed her left breast. There had been no adverse reaction from Katrina, except when he had tried to slip off her brassiere shoulder strap. Then her elbow had moved and clamped his arm tight, forcing him to abandon his attempt to fill his hand with hot molten lava.

"James, do you have any change for the toll?" Her voice was strangled, and he detected just a hint of panic in the tone.

Her request brought him back from his stupor, and he was surprised to find that he was nearly in the driving seat with her, as they descended the slope that ran down to the bridge.

Katrina paid the small charge with a shaking hand. It had taken all her concentration to drive that short journey given the effect her passenger was having on her. Across the road a young couple walked close together, and as the sun gave out its last ray of the day it briefly highlighted the face of the girl. Katrina could see the sheen as clearly as if it had been written on her forehead—she was in love. From the bridge it was only a brief quarter-of-a-mile drive to the canal, but in that short distance of empty road he had been like a bee round a honey pot. Her legs felt like jelly, and as she felt one finger start to trace the outline of her briefs and follow the vee downward towards her inner thigh she could not even protest, only sigh, and miss a gear.

They pulled into the large car park behind the inn, and James wanted to get out of the car as fast as he could—the restraints of the small seat were restrictive, to say the least.

Quickly he moved to help Katrina, almost pulling her bodily upwards as she seemed not to have the strength to move. There were other people in the vicinity, so he was only holding her, and she was glad to hold him tightly, taking deep breaths as she tried to regain some composure. Together they walked slowly hand in hand, as if there was no hurry, but each longed for a quiet place with no one but themselves. Then they came to some steps that led up the canal bank's slope, and there he kissed her hungrily, as if to light the fuse. There was no need—Katrina returned his passion with equal ardour. Two mallards burst from the bank disturbed by the couple passing, leaving wide arrows in their wake on the still water. Then as the disturbance reached the broad tall leaves of the reed clumps, they seemed to bow towards them. Yet neither gave the disturbed troubled water more than a fleeting glance, for their eyes were only for each other. James knew where he was going; they had turned right at the top of the steps, and now they were closing in on the small bridge that spanned the water. Narrow was the path beneath the arch, but there was just enough room to crush her against the stonework and still leave enough space for a passer-by. The runner saw the couple almost blocking his passage; ten miles of his twelve-mile schedule was already completed, so wearily he slowed and called a greeting. Two wide green eyes stared into his face from the girl pressed against the wall, and in that brief glance all his weariness seemed to disappear and he felt completely rejuvenated.

Katrina wanted to scream that there was something brushing her leg but her lips were locked into his so no sound would came out. He felt her jump and try to pull away, then the tail of a dog beat a greeting against his knee. Reluctantly his hands drew away from the warmth of her body, and as they looked they saw a large black labrador wagging a greeting and looking up at them intently. From a distance a voice called loudly, "Come on, Apple, come here." They watched as the overweight dog waddled off. "Good boy, Apple, good boy."

They just stared at each other for a few seconds before almost collapsing with laughter. "Apple," he gasped.

Katrina wiped the tears from her eyes. It was funny, but they had been interrupted twice in a very short time, and all his ardour had almost disappeared with those few words. More like a fat pig, than a dog, she felt herself start to shake with laughter again, then managed to control her mirth.

Across the canal, lights were shining from the large houses dotted along the bank—even these seemed like an intrusion now. Katrina moved into his arms, but he shook his head, and then pointed back the way they had come. Then she grabbed him violently and pulled him the other way, so they walked without a word being spoken until a stone stile gave them access to a field beyond. Katrina knew that once she left the safety of the canal path, she would be committing herself completely to his desires. James helped her over the obstacle, and to her mind they had crossed the dividing line together. All she wanted now was his undivided attention and with no interruptions. Quickly they found a spot and she lay full length submissively. Within minutes, their feverish passion for each other rose unchecked by any intrusion, his mouth burned into hers, and his body was hard and tense like a coiled spring. Tightly she held him as his hand moved under her shoulder blades, his fingers fumbling with the catch on her bra, refusing to release under his inexperienced probing.

There were no words spoken, as she levered herself off the ground and unlocked the two taut full hard throbbing mounds into his eagerly waiting hands. Then she heard him moan, as her nipples hardened under his soft caress, now fully exposed to the evening sky, Then his mouth came onto her rounded flesh, and as his tongue moved across her skin to what he sought, every nerve-end came alive with its contact. Then the shock came as his teeth nibbled and held her nipple briefly, before drawing the hard cherry in and holding it tightly within his lips. Flashes rocketed through her body and into her brain, and her whole self pushed into him urgently as she waited passionately for fulfilment.

Gasping, he reached for the buckle of her trouser belt, and he felt her body arch up towards him and wriggle free, to leave his fingers on her silky white briefs. Gently his hand slipped between her open thighs and he felt the soft raised down beneath. His body quivered uncontrollably. Katrina felt the power surging through him as all the muscles in his body seemed to grow and intensify while his probing fingers sent electric shocks through them both. Almost savagely, the elastic top of her last line of defence was pushed away, giving him free access to her milk-white naked thighs. There was no need to enter, for, as his hand grasped the wet dark secret place, she climaxed, and when it came it blew her mind out of reality. The whole of her body was a mass of electric pulses; then he moved across her and she felt him pause momentarily before entering her inner sanctum. As he tentatively probed within, the moving thunder between them shot bolts of lightning into her head, blotting out everything except the rhythmic movement of their bodies. Then his whole frame seemed to knot like whipcord, as she felt him hold back for a second. But her thighs holding the stallion in check gripped him tightly and pulled him further into her pleasure zone. Great gasps came from him as he drove deeper and every part of his body shook as he exploded within her. Then she matched his passion till they were utterly exhausted and lay quietly together.

Katrina felt his soft breathing on her neck and she shuddered—to her even that was an invitation for more pleasure. How long had they lain together? Ten minutes, an hour? Opening her eyes, Katrina froze, as in the half-light eight huge pairs of unblinking luminous globes stared back at her. Shaking her lover, she laughed and pointed to the four large heads that were looking down at them quizzically. James rolled off, and stood up, then shooed them away making a great play that he was the master although they were only milking cows. Then he grinned, as he thought of how many other couples like themselves had been interrupted or had had an uninvited audience as they tried to make love under the stars. Only then, now that his emotions were under complete control, could he lie down beside her again. No words had been spoken, not that any were needed.

His love for her was overwhelming, and now that they had made love, he was almost frightened by the stupendous magnitude of passion they had created between them.

The lights of the inn shone bright in the darkness as they walked, arms around each other, towards its welcome. Volcanic passion still simmered within the two of them, and she knew that as the night was young the possibility of another intense encounter with its inevitable conclusion was almost one hundred per cent certain.

They paused outside as Katrina closed up the first three buttons of her wool garment, and made sure that there were no pieces of grass sticking to her outer attire. Smiling sweetly, she adjusted his shirt collar as if it was the most natural thing to do, then opened the door for him.

"James, I must phone home."

"Okay, what would you like to drink?"

"Dry white wine, please, I won't be long."

The place was not crowded as yet, so, carrying his pint of bitter and Katrina's glass, he walked towards the large fireplace where there were some empty seats. Two large gulps of best went down smoothly as he sat in the corner waiting for her return.

Reluctantly pressing the digits, she felt completely devoid of reality. On the grass bank all reasoning had been completely blown away as she had become engulfed in the passion that had overwhelmed her. Katrina felt a surge of powerful emotion run through her body. She knew that even now he was waiting for later that night, and his needs and desires were hers also.

Looking at her watch, she hummed a tune. It was only just gone eight; then her connection came.

"Richard Chambers."

She smiled into the mouthpiece. "It's Katrina, tell Mother I will be home late."

"No you won't, Kid, you had better get your pretty ass home here smart-ish, as fast as you can, where are you?"

"The George Inn by the Avon and Kennet Canal, whatever is the matter?"

Katrina began to feel troubled. A chill ran up her spine as a surge of cool air invaded the bar as someone walked in the door from outside.

"You with that new guy?"

"Yes I am." How did her brother know who she was with? It was a secret. Then a feeling of apprehension began to creep slowly over her.

"Katrina, are you still there?"

"Yes, Richard," she replied in a weak voice, "tell me it's not Kelly, he is all right?"

"No it's not your precious horse, you're the one who is in deep trouble."

"Please, what have I done? Richard!"

"Well my lovely, Charles has had a fit, your mother's taking the flack, Joe thinks it's hilarious, and I reckon you and me will have to have a very, very, long talk."

"Richard?" The light flashed and she fumbled frantically for some more change. All passion had fled from her body to be replaced by a feeling of anguish. Two ten-pence pieces dropped down noisily, they were still connected.

Richard spoke softly. "Your, what's his name?"

"James, that's his name," she said defiantly.

"And you, Kiddo were on the tele' this evening, do you want it in graphic detail? And Rodrick has called at home with a proposal of marriage and an engagement ring—your mother is going potty."

Katrina tried to compose her thoughts but nothing would lock into place; her throat felt dry, and it took a lot of effort to reply.

"On television?"

"That's right, the football match—jumping up and down, showing everything you've got, and that kiss, Kiddo."

This shook her to the core—they had only been together for a few hours. Now it had come out into the open for all to see, and she felt a feeling of dread creep over her. Her brother broke in again on her thoughts: "Any plans you may have had for later, you—" The sentence was never finished.

"Katrina—" the word came through loud and clear as if it was shouted, "—I want you home this minute, young lady, do you hear? Your mother and I want a word with you, how could you make such a spectacle of yourself? Home now!"

James played idly with his almost empty glass as he waited patiently for her return. Timber logs burned brightly in the large grate, and as their outer shells were consumed by the flames they rolled together sending myriads of sparks cascading upwards. His gaze focused on the large glass case above the fireplace which held a large stuffed predatory pike, and he mouthed the written words: "Twenty-seven pounds, 1918, River Ely." They were beginning to serve meals and the appetising smell of the food made him feel hungry—if his love agreed, they could eat now.

James stood up to look for Katrina; he had made a promise to himself and the cold-eyed fish above his head that as from this moment his love for her would change his ways. From a distance he could already see the change. Gone was the aureole around the light hair, the sun-kissed face was ashen, and, as his love moved nearer, he saw the sparkle in her eyes which had fired him only a short time ago was dampened. Katrina sat down limply, her fingers intertwining with his. As she looked at him, a sparkle briefly rekindled itself—it was as though someone had struck a match, then, as if blown out by the wind, it was extinguished as suddenly as it had flared.

"I do love you so, James, so much that it hurts." A

small tear trickled down her cheek. Gently he brushed it away with one finger, and softly tried to catch the next one the same way.

"Whatever is the matter, why are you suddenly so unhappy?" He sat down heavily and pulled her in close so that his strength might transfer to her. "Have I upset you in any way? Who were you talking to on the phone?"

James felt a emptiness in his stomach, and panic started to close in for he was thinking that somehow his plans for the rest of the evening had been mind-read by his love and rejected. Katrina saw the pain he felt for her and the look of desperation on his face. She knew the path that both of them had taken was fraught with danger, but she had been more than willing to share that road. Now a few muttered words on a telephone had killed her passage towards greater heights this evening stone dead.

Why should they intrude and interfere in her life, what was it to do with them? Damn them all—well maybe not Richard, he would be on her side?

"James, I am sorry, I must go home now."

"What for, what is the matter?" He gripped her hand tightly in frustration.

Katrina felt a strange feeling of anger and rage build up within her against her mother and father, Why was keeping up appearances more important than her freedom to do whatever she wanted?

"The football match, they showed highlights on the television and my family saw us together, kissing."

The words that his love uttered did not seem to him of any consequence; he was on the tele at the match with the girl of his dreams for everyone to see. It was brilliant! In that few seconds of his own selfish sense of importance he had forgotten that Katrina was leaving him.

"Great, bloody great!" As soon as he had uttered the words he knew it was a mistake. What a clot! He saw her eyes narrow, and her lips move into a thin line. Then he blushed scarlet, and in that instant she forgave him completely.

"Father is furious with me. James, we must go. I will drive you out to the farm."

Katrina wanted to tell him about Rodrick but this was not the time. He would know that she was a virgin before this evening, but would he understand how someone could ask her to marry him if they were not close?

Their return was measured in minutes, not like the hours that it had taken them to reach this point, and, although his passion still stirred beneath the surface, his seat belt was firmly locked in place, and, as they drove in silence, he stared from the car window with blank unseeing eyes. Katrina just went through the motions of driving: all her physical feelings were just in a blank empty shell now, and the nearer to their destination they got, the more depressed she became.

"Shall I phone you later, Katrina?"

"No, I will call," she answered in a whisper. "Tomorrow around noon."

Their parting was swift—just a quick peck as he moved out from his seat, but he tasted salt on his lips and knew that she had been, or was, crying in the darkness of the car, he could not tell which.

"Damn it, I will follow you down."

"No, please, I will see you tomorrow, I promise," she pleaded. "James—"

He paused, hoping that there had been a change of mind and that they would go together. He felt her hands on his neck. "I love you so much that it hurts, you do believe that?" Her voice came soft and full of emotion, so that a lump came into his throat almost choking him.

Slumping into the driver's seat of his Escort, he watched the red tail lights disappear into the darkness bearing with it his hopes for the future. Then he began to work out with a love-clouded yet logical mind the pluses and minuses of the day. Most important he had met and become completely besotted by the girl of his dreams; he was totally and overwhelmingly in love. They had both been on the television highlights; that was a plus—he was sure that his father would have seen it and most of his mates, and that would give him something to crow about when he saw them later. The local professional team were interested in his ability as a goalkeeper. He grinned: they must be struggling! The training would be hard but at least it would make him fitter and with the cutting-down on his cigarettes and beer, there would be a few more pounds left in his pocket at the end of the week.

Then there was her riding: if Katrina was as good as his father implied, most of her waking time would be spent with Kelly. Not that horses frightened him, but he always felt safer with a hedge or fence between them and himself when coin-searching. What if Katrina asked him to go riding with her? There could only be one answer: if you want me to die young, lead on.

His mates at the local would give him a hard time when they knew that he was going out with a horse rider; there were sure to be many rude comments concerning his performance in the saddle, but he would have to take the jibes, and maybe just stretch their imagination a little.

When he had seen her from the ridge in the morning, just to speak to her would have been enough, and maybe next time ask her out. How was he to know that passion of this magnitude blows away all sense of reasoning, and that once you light the touch paper you can be consumed in pillars of fire. His reflected face on the glass stared back at him and he realised that his transport was stationary in the drive of his home. There was no recollection of the homeward journey, and he realised that it was pure instinct that had propelled the car to this place without his knowing how it got there.

Getting out of the seat, his decision was not to go across to the local straightaway but let his mates sweat a little longer. If they had seen the two of them on the sports programme all sorts of rumours would be circulating around the public bar. James opened the front door with his key. On hearing his entry, the dog barked a greeting from the another room, then it came running, wagging its tail furiously. "Candy, Candy, have you missed me, you silly dog?"

"James, is that you?"

"Mother, who do you want, Father Christmas?"

"There is some ham in the fridge if you're hungry?"

For the first time that day he realised he was starving: a couple of sandwiches at the football ground, and a pint of bitter at the inn had been his total intake for the day, unless—he grinned—I wonder how many calories there are in love-making? Because in that case he had had a bellyful.

Wholemeal bread was already cut for him, and, as the water boiled to make the coffee, he amused himself by feeding broken biscuits to his four-legged companion. Munching his sandwich ravenously and taking tentative sips from his cup, with his follower close behind, at last he walked in to the room where his mother and father were sitting. The very first thing that he noticed—and it was so obvious, almost laughable—the television volume was muted.

"You're home early, dumped you, has she?"

Nearly taking the bait that was offered by his father, but letting the jibe go at the last minute, he replied in a voice without any outward emotion, "No, Katrina's brother is down from London, and he's going back in the morning."

"Were you at the match? They won two nil, it was on the box, your mother and I watched the highlights."

Another question, yet the answer already known—so they had seen both of them together.

"Yes, Dad, we were at the game as you well know, so let's drop it, can we?"

James fed the dog the last few crumbs from his plate then got up to go out.

A softer voice spoke: "James, be careful with the young lady."

"Yes, Mother, I promise. By the way, Dad, when I was at the ground they asked if I was interested in playing again, a couple of the keepers are injured."

"Tell me more," he replied, now alert.

James shook his head. "Not now, I want to go out."

His mother cut in: "How much have you drunk today?"

He answered honestly, "Only one pint, just one, all right? If I don't go now they will be shut."

James ran all the way; his mind was saying start getting in trim now, run, run, run!

They were waiting for him, as he had guessed rightly, but what he didn't know was how early the rumours had started, and as the evening wore on, and alcohol loosened tongues, the more fantastic were their telling. They had not prolonged their stay at the ground, although with plenty of banter and rude comments all of them except one, and that was Nobby the driver, volunteered to let the girl sit on their lap if by chance they appeared. The news had spread fast: they were the real supporters and they had seen him large as life at the game. A few armchair critics watching the highlights recognised him too. Now even those who had not seen him were participating and speculating in the chatter. James had signed for the team and they were paying him five hundred pounds a match and the girl was the manager's daughter. Then the girl was the chairman's niece, and on good authority, Miss Bristol, and as he was such a bastard his money was eight hundred a week. Beer was going down a treat, it was gone ten and he still had not arrived. Nobby looked across at one of his mates, and in a slightly slurred voice said, "What did you s'say, goldee lock's iss Misss World, and that s'sod is in goal next game? I'm not going."

The reporter waited patiently. He had also been at the match and had seen the couple, but after the game was over had been unable to glean who the young man was. Now it seemed his luck may have changed. One thing was for sure; he seemed to frequent this pub fairly often, and it was only on a whim that he had dropped in for a quick half of beer. Almost immediately he had picked up on the rumour; now almost an hour had gone by and he was already into his second pint, which was unusual as he hardly drank at all. James turned the door handle to the public bar. It was brass, and as it glowed in the light it fleetingly reminded him of her.

Katrina silenced the engine of her small sports car at the top of the slope, then let it run silently into her parking space. She sat for a brief moment to gather her thoughts.

Inside she was seething with rage, but it was a controlled fury and she knew that when her father started to grill her about what she'd been doing, which at the match was so innocent, she would be ready to give as good as she got. Her overwhelming love for James had made her much stronger. In only their short time together she knew that there would never ever be anyone else, and she would fight now and in the future so that they could share together what was rightfully theirs: each other.

Even if her father had paid thousands of pounds for Kelly, under her guidance and schooling over the last two years, his value had almost doubled.

What price did they expect her to pay, to be called home like a fifteen-year-old? It was degrading, how ever was she going to grow up like her brother, strong and independent? Even before he was eighteen he had left home. Katrina savagely kicked the tyre of her father's car. Why was she still here at twenty? What was she doing now, coming home so early, when all her thoughts were with him?

Soundlessly the dark figure struck as Katrina walked slowly towards the front door. She felt the hand across her mouth but it came so fast that even if she had wanted to scream no sound would have come. Her body was pinned securely against her attacker as he easily lifted her from the floor and back towards the parked cars. Although she tried to struggle the clamp-like grip paralysed her.

"Katrina, it's Richard," a voice whispered in her ear,

"don't make a noise." Gently he lowered her to the ground.

The atmosphere in the house was tense so he had walked into the garden to clear his mind, and from a distance across the rolling fields he had heard a car, and with his training came a built-in ability gained over the years to isolate individual sounds. As it came nearer he knew it was his sister's.

"Stand up for yourself, remember, Kiddo, Joe and I are on your side. Give me a few minutes, then come in, no one will have heard you."

Then he was gone as quickly as he had appeared. Just a flicker of light from the front door was all that betrayed his passing, no rasp of a key or a scuff of a shoe. She knew that her brother could be deadly, and he had frightened her. Katrina bent down, then got down on her knees—her small handbag had tumbled from her grasp when Richard had manhandled her, now its contents were scattered on the floor in a heap.

"What ever are you doing?" came a loud voice directly above her head. "Come on in, your father's waiting for you, young lady."

The first thing that Katrina noticed was the two red spots, one on each side of his face, and the flushed look of anger.

"What have you to say for yourself?" The words were almost spat out. Katrina felt her body turn slightly as if to walk out of the room, but she steeled herself, gritted her teeth, tilted her chin and looked him directly in the eye defiantly.

"You did not tell your mother that you were going to a football match this afternoon, did she, Catherine? Making a spectacle of yourself, half-naked in front of all those people." His eyes became slits as he paused for breath.

Richard spoke, and she knew that he would try to lower her father's anger, "Hey Kiddo, if you had told me you were going to the game, maybe Joe and me would have come," and he winked without anyone noticing.

Katrina went to answer, but her father had not finished. "Look at you, almost undressed!"

The buttons on her cardigan had popped when Richard had grabbed her in the darkness. Without thinking she had just pulled it together, now it gaped wide open at the front to show her bare flesh. Nothing her father had asked even merited a reply, his questions so trivial.

"Who is this *boy*?" The words came from her mother, with the emphasis on boy, as if James was a nonentity.

"You've never mentioned him before; it was disgusting, that fellow kissing and mauling you in front of all those people, we saw it."

Katrina had not yet spoken in defence of her actions, but when her mother, unwittingly or not, said boy with such demeaning overtones, she felt an inner steeliness of cold, grey anger sweep over her. They should not ever talk of the most precious thing in the world to her like that. Horse, car, family, they all paled into nothingness compared with him. Picking her reply carefully and turning towards her mother, she spoke softly but with power and conviction.

"His name is James, and he called me lunch-time. He did not maul me as you put it, and I gave him a kiss in the excitement of the game, and I will be seeing him again."

George spoke with a threat in his voice: "Well, young lady, you will not be going to a football match next week, that's for sure, and if I have my way, never. Only complete dedication without any distractions will get you to the top; your horse Kelly cost me a stack of money, are you going to throw it all away?"

He knew the last words would hurt, but it was for her own good; his daughter was not going out with anyone who might interfere with his ultimate goal—her inclusion in the Olympic Squad.

Katrina's face dropped, and her father, watching closely, saw that the barb had struck deep. His countenance took on a half-smile as he sat back in the chair contentedly.

Then she knew what to say: it was almost as if across the night sky which separated their bodies, he had communicated with her inner soul and whispered the pearls of wisdom. "James is a friend, just a casual acquaintance."

Then she swallowed and looked embarrassed. Richard stared at her wide-eyed; he knew that she was lying, but Father seemed to believe her, so what?

"How did you meet the young man, Katrina, does he live near the village?" her mother asked lightly.

Two questions with straightforward answers: her body felt less tense as she replied, "In the valley, Mother. James comes with his father from Bristol—they search for coins." His name had rolled off her tongue so sweetly that she almost blushed with shame, and had to avert her eyes for a few seconds to compose herself.

George made a mental note to have a word with Alan. Even if he paid rent for his land, it was not in his interest for outsiders to dig holes in his garden, big as it was.

"Rodrick came to the house; he was not sure if you were going to walk the course with him this afternoon?"

"I told him to phone the farm, but unfortunately when he arrived you had gone." That was her mother's probe, hoping that she would give some hint or even a gesture of her feelings for him.

Katrina did not reply as her father spoke. "It took me five hours to drive down from Manchester today. There were two accidents both involving caravans that caused chaos with the traffic—they should never be allowed on the motorway. Your mother spoke to him, as you can guess, I was sat going nowhere. How many times has he phoned since, Catherine?"

Katrina unconsciously ran a finger across her forehead and traced the scar. Although it was almost four years ago that the swishing branch had almost blinded her, except for the white blemish there had been a complete recovery. Richard noted the change in his father's tone, and as Katrina had surmised also, he had not completely forgiven him for the damage to his daughter.

"Well, only twice, why don't you give Rodrick a call later, dear? You could arrange to meet tomorrow." Her tone was not convincing, and the look on her daughter's face suggested that her words were falling on deaf ears.

The atmosphere in the room was a lot easier now and when Josie asked if she should make a pot of tea, they all answered in the affirmative. Katrina breathed a sigh of relief as her father and mother followed her into the large adjoining kitchen. Only her brother was left, and he was moving closer to her with a quizzical look on his face. "Tell me about James? *He* is more than your friend? I reckon he is your..."

He left the word unspoken, but her look betrayed all.

❦

Through the clear glass they saw him turning the handle of the door, and a cheer went up as he stepped inside to a hero's welcome, and he revelled in it. A drink was placed on one of the tables and a chair appeared, although there had not been any empty before he had walked in. They were all speaking at once and the reporter only picked up snatches of information above the hubbub. The person of their attention was a goalkeeper. This did not surprise him in the least as he knew of the spate of injuries.

Sitting back comfortably, he waited for the noise to subside and for his chance to move nearer, he was trying to listen for words which were repeated often. Katrina—

he got that and mentally stored it away; Badminton, that was next week. Buying another beer he started to build up a picture from what he had heard.

"Jamer, are you coming down town?"

"No thanks, count me out."

"Bloody hell, James, you really do mean to train tomorrow! If this is what it does to you I don't want to know, come on."

Let them think what they want, he had already told them more than enough. Now all he needed was to be alone with his thoughts for the future. They waved as they tumbled out into the car park, laughing and joking at his expense, and most threw in a few two-fingered signs for good measure.

One, as he went out, shouted through the door, "Stuck-up bastard," but he was grinning, and the seated figure did not take offence.

Swiftly the stranger at the bar moved and sat down in the still warm seat vacated directly opposite.

"You want a beer, young man?"

James looked up, his hair bristling. Was this guy trying to pick him up?

The reporter sensed the mood, and spoke quickly, "Saw you at the match, good result, what did you think?"

"No not bad, should have had four at least."

"Play a bit of football yourself, do you?"

James nodded.

"Your mates say that you've signed on, is that right?" More questions, who was he? What business was it of his anyway?

"Don't go, I'm a reporter, just local, not big league, football mostly, I'm a fan of the team, same as you." Crystal clear, the words were uttered, in short precise blocks, so there was no mistaking the message.

James looked at him more closely. He was around his father's age, but with a kind face that made him feel more comfortable. A reporter and interviewing me—he sipped his pint thoughtfully; maybe he had seen Katrina ride.

"That young lady you were with, is she your fiancée?"

He laughed. "No, my girlfriend." He did not divulge that they had only met for the first time that day.

"Can you tell me her full name? Your mates were telling me that you are going out with one of the directors' daughters, is that right? And that you have signed on?"

"That's it, I'm going now. Her name is Katrina Chambers and the horse's name is Kelly, I start training tomorrow."

James walked slowly out of the bar into the night air, covering the short distance to his home in minutes. So much had gone on throughout the day that he felt overwhelmed with its enormity. Then he grimaced. Tomorrow? What would it bring? Hard graft at the training ground in the morning, but he could look forward with anticipation to the afternoon. Then a cloud blotted out the moon as if it were a black omen. What of Katrina's protective family, would they try and stop her seeing him again?

Katrina busied herself around the house. She knew that when the washing-up was finished her mother would come and question her again. Her first idea was to go to her room and lock the door, but that was only running away. George had retired to his study on the pretext of writing a letter, and Josie and Richard were in the process of going for a walk in the garden. That left her mother conveniently placed to talk to her without any interference from anyone. There was not long to wait. As soon as the front door closed, her mother came towards her with hands outstretched—just like James had when they met in the stable yard, but there was no fire or feeling in them, not like his.

"Shall we sit by the window, dear? It's more cosy there."

Katrina walked across the room and sat down on the far side of the sofa, crossing her legs and waiting for her mother's questions.

"No, nearer, dear, not right over there."

Katrina moved a few inches closer.

"You know your father only wants the best for you, we all do. How long have you known this young man? You have never confided in me—where does he live?"

Lots of questions without any rancour: this could be used to her advantage. The gap narrowed as Catherine moved closer.

"Mother, his name is James Eagles and he comes from the outskirts of Bristol."

"You do not know exactly?"

Katrina shook her head.

"How long have you been seeing him?"

"Ages," she lied. "He comes with his father on a Saturday morning, detecting for coins. He asked if I would like to go to a football match as he had a spare ticket." This was not true, but her inner voice kept saying, "Tell them what they want to hear."

"You must like him a lot, as we saw on the television."

Katrina laughed and closed the gap completely between them. "That was just excitement: remember when you jumped up and down and danced on the tow path with a perfect stranger when Richard's crew won the boat race. I know that feeling now, Mother."

Catherine felt the colour rise in her cheeks. How strong was her daughter's memory to remember that incident. George had not been with them that day and he'd been a handsome young man—now all these years later she has come up with this comparison as if it had happened only yesterday.

Catherine tried to get her thoughts in order. Her daughter had neatly turned everything around, now she was speaking again, and she wished George would reappear.

Katrina saw the slight doubt in her mother's eyes but there was no pity in hers. She had been humiliated and treated like a child, not a woman in her own right. Then the brief surge of red rage subsided as quickly as it had come. There was always tomorrow for her and the path was already mapped out, whatever they said.

"Mother, we only went for a walk after the game, then we went in the George on the canal to order a meal. It was so embarrassing when Father ordered me home, why?"

Katrina lay back puzzled. Her father had spoken with anger, but Mother seemed almost as if she were just going through the motions without any real conviction at all. There was something else.

"We both love you a lot, and we want you to be happy, but it was a great shock to your father, and Rodrick also phoned to ask what was going on?"

"Rodrick, that creep!" She spat out the words with all the venom she could muster. Wherever in the country Kelly and she were competing, he would turn up, spotted face, lean as a rake—he looked older than her brother although she knew that he was only twenty-two. Now her mother had given her the missing piece to the jigsaw! When exercising her stallion in the valley he would appear like a bad dream, flattering and trying to touch her body; he made her feel sick. Over the last month or so he had called fairly often on the pretext that he was just passing. He was a good rider, she would grant him that, and his father's estate was huge.

"Would you like a nice apple, dear?" Apple, apple… Suddenly she was under the arch by the canal, and she felt the long bones of his fingers rasp across her silky smooth skin, and the face of Rodrick leered down as her whole body went ridged with shock. It was to awful to even contemplate.

"Mother, you can tell Father that he is always trying to pinch my bottom and fondle my breasts when we are together."

Catherine sat bolt upright, and put her hand over her mouth. What had started out as a sharp reminder to her daughter as to her station in life, and a homily that keeping up appearances and standards were paramount, for the sake of the family, had now completely degenerated. The conversation was out of her control.

"Touch you?"

"Yes, Mother, but don't worry on my behalf. I have more than put him in his place."

Katrina felt much better. She had slightly exaggerated Rodrick's actions, but lately his hands had seemed to wander into unsought places as he helped her dismount.

Catherine sat pondering; her daughter was growing up fast, maybe too fast for George and her to handle.

"Hey Kiddo, has Mother been telling you about the birds and the bees?" Richard was standing in the doorway looking directly at her, and she could have killed him there and then.

"Mother, would you like to see the hotel where we will be staying?

"Katrina, be a dear, go and find your father, so we can all look together."

"Yes, Mother." She walked to his study door and knocked; everyone in the family always tapped, even Richard. She had often wondered what her father did in there, and now, awaiting his call, it seemed as if she was outside the door of a headmaster's room, not her father's.

"Come in. Oh, it's you, Katrina, has your mother had a word?

"Yes, Father." She felt drained, surely not more questions again.

"So it's settled then. You will not be so headstrong in the future, your mother and I know what's best for you."

On the table lay an open address book, and, as her father flicked it shut, she saw that the name of Rodrick was clearly underlined. So that was his game! She smiled inwardly not letting any emotion show that she had scanned the page. When her mother told him later of Rodrick's sexual advances, that would really give him something to worry about.

"By the way what do you want, can I help?"

"Richard has the holiday stuff, well no, his honeymoon really. He asked if you would come so that we can all look at it together."

“This is the deal: we all fly out on Tuesday week in the morning from Gatwick.”

“Richard, how much is it going to cost you?” Catherine queried.

“Look, Mother, please don’t interrupt!” He pointed to a map of the island: “We will be staying on the famous St James Coast and the wedding is at the Hotel Royal Pavilion right on the beach. This is where all of us will be staying until the wedding. Then Joe and I will be flying on to Antigua for our honeymoon. Bring the tennis rackets, Katrina, and here is some spending money for you—it’s my treat, though I’ll want it back if you win Badminton, mind.” They all laughed.

Katrina was busy reading the page of the brochure and the name James stood out like a beacon. Was it just a coincidence that they were staying on a shore line with his name to remind her of their love for each other?

Badminton was looming up in a few days’ time, and now there was her brother’s wedding to think about—both important in their own right, but what of tomorrow? What if he kissed her and she knew he would? Katrina felt weak at her thoughts; it was getting late and there was a lot to do in the morning; Kelly, her second love, would be waiting and ready.

“Goodnight, I want to be up early. Are you staying for the rest of the week, Richard?”

“No, we are going back in the morning, but we will

drive down on Thursday to see you ride, okay? By the way, don't forget, see you before we leave?"

Katrina blushed, she knew what he wanted her for—it would be no good lying to him.

George did not see his daughter leave the room, but he was glad that she had gone. Now the four of them could think of some plan to stop her seeing this stranger, so putting her whole future at risk through his distraction.

Richard shuffled the papers as his father walked towards where he was sitting. He knew that their topic of conversation would be his sister so he took the initiative and spoke first. "Now we are all together, and both of you have spoken to—" He gestured towards the ceiling. "—What are your plans? Father?"

George cleared his throat. "Stop it before it goes any further."

"Mother?"

"I agree, your father has spent thousands. Now Katrina has reached the top grade I do not think that any distractions are good for her, now or in the future, especially with someone we don't know."

"Well I believe you're both wrong. Katrina is headstrong, brave and physically sexually aroused. Don't 'kill it' or you may regret your actions for the rest of your life. This young man is more important to her *now*, at this minute, than anything else in the world. Please let her go her own way for the sake of us all."

The orator looked up grim-faced, and they were all

looking at him in stunned silence, every word he'd uttered had come straight from the heart.

Catherine looked with embarrassment at her husband who was standing stony-faced; usually Richard only spoke in short clipped words with a grin or smile, but this time he had been deadly serious.

Richard had not quite finished, though he felt more relaxed since what he was going to say next was more directed at Josie whose help he might need when he spoke to his sister in the morning.

"Joe and myself will speak to Katrina before we go, I promise." Then he laughed. "Don't look so downhearted, Father, it will turn out for the best—you'll see."

Josie was staring at her future husband—for a small doubt troubled her mind. Did Richard love his sister more than her? Then she dismissed this instantly as he kissed her forcibly on the lips.

"Come on, let's hit the stairs."

The figure of their conversation was curled up in a ball, dreaming sweet thoughts, and in this half-sleep where all things are possible, she had floated with her love back to the still dark water of the canal, now shimmering in the moonlight under a bright star-spangled sky.

Deep in the suburbs, the bright glow of a half-finished cigarette was extinguished as it was ground into the dust by a heavy heel. The house was in darkness, and the night watchman only raised a pointed head briefly.

No growl or bark broke the stillness, and when the intruder entered and made no move to scratch his belly, he snuggled down and went back to sleep.

James cleaned his teeth, dropped his shirt, pants and socks into the washing basket, washed himself, hung his trousers on a hanger, not in the usual crumpled heap on the floor, then fell in to bed.

God, he felt knackered, what a day, what a hell of a day!

The goalkeeper was up early for a Sunday; the time was only eight o'clock. Usually if he made it by eleven that was good; most of the time it would be around midday, a quick couple of slices of toast, then up to the local for a few pints. Spread out on the floor was his complete kit, including his boots which were clean and polished. He knew that his father must have preceded his awakening by at least an hour. The morning work-out would be hard, and something inside said don't bother, it's not worth the hassle. Then he thought of the girl, his girl—if Katrina could be a winner, why not him?

The rider was up at daybreak, long before her love. There were things to do at the yard and this would be the last sortie in the valley with Kelly. Tomorrow morning, the horse would be transported the short distance to the stables at Badminton.

Katrina walked into the bathroom slowly. All was quiet in the house. Her face looked a little pale in the early dawn light but she knew that within a short time the wind would flush her cheeks to a golden glow. Fifteen minutes later she drove into the stable yard and parked her car. The horse was waiting impatiently, and so were half a dozen of her stable companions. This was unusual, so early in the morning.

Alan walked over. "Everything all right?"

"Yes, he looks fine."

"Go on, ask her," a squeaky voice cried. "Go on."

The small group came closer. "Is that right, Katrina? You were on the television, who is that fellow? We want to know!" they all chorused in unison.

The rider had not given much thought to love when she had risen; now a small tingle slowly began to build. Could she contemplate taking a ride on the roller-coaster today? Katrina started to mount as they gathered round, not too close now that she sat astride Kelly. The stallion snorted, as she spoke to him softly.

"Come on, tell us!"

"Just a friend, only a friend." The lie came out so easily! Why was she saying this? How many more fibs would she have to tell because of a few stupid seconds on the television?

"But I saw you kiss him, I did, I did," came the same voice with a passion as great as if she'd been the recipient.

Katrina felt the sweat run down her face; she wanted to be alone. Her mind began to flash back to her love near the canal, then forward to the stable yard—warm, cold, hot, cold, red searing heat as he took her completely. A great shudder went through her body as she gripped the horse tightly. Blindly, she forced her way through the crowd and made her way into the arena with her faithful flock watching intently.

Kelly sensed that his rider was not totally in command as they went through the routines and disciplines of the dressage. To a casual observer, the pair looked magnificent, set like a statue in bronze as if the two of them were one. Katrina was only going through the motions this morning, and it seemed that, no matter how hard she tried to concentrate, her best was not nearly good enough.

"Blast!" she swore at the horse as he made another elementary error. Kelly snorted; it was his rider who was mixed up, not him. They stood around in silence, just watching. They had followed, hoping for more titbits, but now they were praying that one day they could emulate the pair, and earn the invite to compete at Badminton. Time this morning was not important, so again Kelly and Katrina went through the tough routine. Then suddenly, as when scenting a single-stemmed rose, when the senses are focused within the heart of its beauty, and the fragrance takes your breath away, in one instant Katrina knew that this was the moment. There in a field with only a handful of avid watchers they had reached perfection.

"Good boy, good boy," was all she could say, as with tears streaming down her face she walked past the silent awe-struck watchers. She moved on, taking a gentle hack down the slope towards the valley and peace, with a long snake of followers strung out behind her like beads on a chain. Rodrick was nowhere to be seen, and she laughed out loud as the spirit of the beauty of the valley elevated her. A hare bolted from its cover, yet Kelly did not flinch. Many a time he had run with these furry creatures, and this morning it would be no different.

"Whoa, whoa, slow down," she called as he tried to break into a stride. "Come on, boy, save your strength for later in the week."

Alan watched Katrina ride into the yard, watching her talking to him softly, and patting his nose to try and calm his strength, untapped by the morning's ride.

"Ready, is he?"

Katrina turned round. "Yes, he's fine, just fine."

"How do you reckon, this week?"

"If we get into the top twenty, I will be happy," she went on, rubbing him down carefully as Alan walked away.

The rider had already forgotten that the owner of the stable had set her up yesterday, and so had he. Although it would not be long before he would know that the two of them had met, overhearing gossip as other horses deposited their riders who were all chattering and giving Katrina adoring looks.

James sat on the grass, away from the other players, loosening up. He had fully kitted himself up before he had left home except for his boots; now he was tying the laces. The trainer smiled. "Still the same loner," he said almost silently as he walked over to the half-prone figure. Another fine morning was forecast with temperatures still in the sixties and no chance of rain that day. James spat on his gloves, crouched down and gave the signal that he was ready.

The ball came just within finger-tip range as he dived full length to the right. Then he was up quickly as the next one came to the left. He had been through this agony many times in the past as his father drove him on to fitness and agility—there was one thing in common with then and now, it hurt. Fifteen minutes of this torture had passed, when he felt it coming up from his stomach in a rush. He scrambled towards the hedge and was violently sick. The ball-thrower waited, then shouted at his charge, "Come on!"

Now the point had been proved, would the keeper respond or walk away?

James retched some more; then in the far distance through water-filled eyes he saw a horse and rider. He would do it for her! Gritting his teeth, he walked back scowling. "Yes, I'll show them!" These comments were only for the wind to hear.

"You all right?"

"Get on with it," he snarled at the grinning face.

Tested he was again, but only for a couple of minutes. This time an inner power drove him effortlessly outwards and upwards so that whatever speed or direction the ball came he seemed to have it covered completely.

"That's enough, James, I'll round up a few players

to give you a real run out." The track-suited trainer walked away to where other figures were passing a football to each other, then gathered them close. Pointing a finger, "That's a new keeper on trial, plenty of action but not too rough, mind, we may need him."

"Doesn't look much to me, boss."

"You'll be surprised. I can tell you from experience that his reactions are so fast that if five flies flew past, he could catch three of them before you moved." He smiled to himself—that sounded original.

"Go at it now, do as I say."

Joining the opposing team, making it seven players to five, he watched intently as balls rained in from all angles at the keeper.

High above the head of one of his own team, James held the ball, only to feel two hands trying to drag him back into the net. As he descended, the object he held came down on an unsuspecting nose. A cry of anguish rent the air and a raised fist was shaken in his direction. He ignored the threat and lashed the ball away, then turned quickly and moved across to the prone figure, who was rubbing his afflicted part.

"There is plenty more where that come from, stay out of my way," he shouted.

The trainer waited patiently, watching the pattern of play, then he began to count out loud, not that anyone could hear—three, two—. Before he reached one, the keeper was off his line and down at the feet of the incoming forward. Clutching the ball firmly in both hands, James felt the boot sear across his face, the pain coming instantly, but to him that did not matter—only that they had not scored.

"Come on, that's enough for today, get washed up."

"You're an animal," the player whined, still rubbing his reddened nose, but he stayed well away from the six-foot-plus keeper.

James turned his head to show the bright blue ridge running from his mouth to his ear. "That's the two of us, it's all in the game."

The phone in the office was ringing, and the trainer picked it up reluctantly. Every time it rang lately, it was bad news. He listened intently to the caller at the same time, looking out of the window as father and son climbed into their transport.

"I don't believe what I'm hearing. How in the hell did you know we might sign on another keeper for emergency cover?"

"Is it true?" the caller asked.

"Well we might—his name is James Eagles."

"I know that," the caller replied.

"You can't. We only had him in this morning; have you bugged the place?" The trainer looked vainly for someone with a mobile phone— no luck with the keeper or his father whom he had seen walk to the car empty-handed.

The caller was still speaking. "Look, all I want is how good is he? Will he play for any of the teams this week?"

Tony cut the caller off, and put the phone down, then looked under the table, in the drawer of the desk, or anywhere a bug could be planted.

6

Josie and Richard were leaning on the gate, waiting as Katrina drove into the drive with a squeal of tyres to park within an inch of her brother's car.

"You drive too fast, Kiddo, are you ready?"

"Can I change first?" she pleaded.

"No, not at all."

Katrina appealed to Josie but to no avail, so the three of them walked off together. For the first twenty strides or more they were silent.

"Josie." Katrina pulled her in close, and slowed, so that her words would not be overheard by her brother.

Then she told her of their walk along the towpath, and the feelings that had erupted. Richard was hopping from side to side, completely shut out of the conversation, and only catching a few words now and again.

"Are you seeing him today?" Josie asked.

"Of course," Katrina replied smiling sweetly.

"What if he tries again?"

"What are you two are talking about?" Richard interrupted.

"Your sister's future, and how to get through this week without any pressure from your mother and father."

"Okay, Kiddo, we will convince the two of them that you are just friends. I know we will be lying, so if anything goes wrong..." He drew his hand across his throat.

Somewhere near the M4 and M32 intersection, the reporter was trying to ring a colleague on his mobile phone, no answer. Already the need to drop into work for an hour on a Sunday had not gone down very well with his wife, Mary.

"No, later, you promised we would go over to Mother's for lunch."

"Yeah, yeah," he replied without any conviction in his voice. Driving into town was easy this morning—no traffic snarl-ups as in the week. Fifteen minutes later, he walked into the main office and sat in front of his computer. Keying in her name, he waited for the information from the library files to scroll up on the screen.

KATRINA CHAMBERS: it listed her address, age, and all her positions in eventing and show jumping to date, and that an invite had been sent for her to compete at Badminton. Jotting the salient points down, he began to type, merging the information on the rider with what he had gleaned from the public bar the night before.

Changing a few words he sat back and scanned the small paragraph:

> One of our Young Top Eventing Riders, Katrina Chambers, is romantically linked with Bath Rangers' new goalkeeper, James Eagles. They were seen together for the first time on Saturday at the home match. Neither of the couple would comment on this budding romance. Supporters of the Rangers wish her well for the Badminton Horse Trials this week, and say that Miss Chambers is welcome to visit the club at any time.

That was it: not much but exclusive. It should make the inside pages at least, and it would put him one up on a colleague whom he knew was covering the horse trials this week.

James wallowed in the hot bath, trying to bring back some life into his limbs. The most disquieting thing was that he had volunteered to repeat this awful dose each day for the next week. On the floor lay his discarded clothes in a bundle, and without thinking he tossed them into the wash basket as he passed. Stumbling to the bedroom with a towel around his middle, he found it was easier to lie on the bed to put on his clean clothes than bend down. That felt better! He pushed himself up and looked in the mirror at his reflection. Not too bad—maybe his eye would not close at all. What would Katrina think of him today, looking as though he had been in a fight? The eiderdown looked inviting—so soft. As a warm breeze came wafting through the open window he suddenly felt terribly tired. James knew that if she called he would hear the phone. Just a few precious minutes' relaxation—not to sleep, but to wait for her call in perfect peace.

A short time later he awoke with a start, and in haste made for the kitchen, where he could hear his mother.

"What's the matter with you?" his mother asked. "That face looks sore, are you sure you didn't get kicked in the head? Do you want your father to take you to the hospital for a check-up?"

James screwed up his face. "Dad, tell Mother not to fuss, and to shut up."

"Oh, I forgot, there was a phone call for you while you were asleep," his father said brightly, then paused as if he had forgotten the name of the caller or any message that might have been left.

"Who was it?" The words came out in a kind of panic.

"It was Curly, said to tell you the bar's open all day."

James tried to control his inner thoughts before replying, "I am, well, might be going out later."

John winked at his wife, making sure that the gesture was noticed by his son. "If you like, you can go up the pub, and when the young lady calls, your mother or me will take a message."

"Go to hell, Dad, I'm not going up there." With that he got up from the table, walked into the garden, lit a cigarette, then worried.

Katrina was ecstatic: whatever her brother and Josie had told her mother and father it had certainly lessened the tension around the house. There was no mention of her misdemeanours of the evening before; all the conversation centred around the forthcoming marriage or the horse trials later in the week. Catherine was already making plans for the three of them to visit Bath to purchase new outfits. Even George realised that a heavy suit was a non-starter in the climate that they would be in.

While they were in jovial conversation, she slipped away. Katrina felt more worried about what to wear today than at her brother's wedding in two weeks' time. Peering into her wardrobe, full of clothes, she took out the mini-skirt that she had discarded the previous day—she really liked the feel of the material, it felt and looked so sexy. The thought went through her mind—suspenders and stockings. Wicked! She felt weak thinking about herself, let alone what her love would make of it. Then she laughed with glee as the garment was discarded once again.

"James would probably burst into flames!"

The choice was obvious—a figure-hugging sweater tucked into slacks tightly belted; there would be no buttons to pop on this outfit. Katrina let her fingers rustle over the material which enclosed what he had desired and caressed the evening before, driving her to the point of madness. Why was her mind constantly on him and what they would do together? When should she phone, with the family watching, how would it be possible?

"How stupid you are," she almost said out loud. The answer was to use the public call box a short distance down the road since she had no mobile. Gathering her purse and making sure that the short, short, skirt was put away safely from her mother's eyes, she made for the bedroom door, turning the handle and opening it wide she startled, as framed in the entrance poised to knock was Richard, with Josie in close attendance.

"Hey Kiddo, we are all going out to lunch, are you coming?"

Katrina pursed her lips—the answer to the question was no, as this would leave her alone to make the call, but would it upset Josie? Just now the further her mother and father stayed away from her the better. As for her brother, eating at the same table would have her on a knife edge just waiting for him to say the wrong words.

Josie saw the look of hesitation on her face so spoke for her. "I know you want to go out, so we'll see you Thursday."

"Thanks, Josie, it's much appreciated. Have a pleasant journey back to London. Richard, tell Mother that I'll be going out, but will be home early this evening."

"Will do," he replied, saluting mockingly.

Katrina counted the minutes as she waited, not daring to go down the stairs or even to the window where someone might see her, and so delay their departure for even a few more moments of idle chatter.

Click went the front door as it shut softly—that was her mother's hand, not the bang of her brother or father. Then came muted voices and the powerful purring sound of the BMW engine bursting into life. Katrina held her breath as the crunch of gravel took on a new meaning—they were gone! She leapt up and twirled around the room, arms held high, and calling to the heavens, "I am free!"

James was sat on the grass throwing the ball for the dog to retrieve. As he stubbed out another cigarette he realised that he was automatically reaching for his lighter to chain-smoke.

"Candy, do you know why Katrina has not called yet?"

The dog pricked up its ears and listened as the speaker ranted on.

"Stuff her father and mother! I'm going to call her, do you agree?" Deep down, he knew that there was nothing that he could do but wait. Yet it made him feel better now it was out of his system, and even his friend was wagging her tail.

Nervously a slim strong hand hovered near the phone. Should she call now, or wait a few minutes to make sure that one of her family had not inadvertently forgotten something, and might return to interrupt her conversation?

"James, James!" The call came from inside the house. In haste he ran with his sleek-coated friend, jumping up in excitement at this new game.

"It's Katrina."

Clenching his fist, "Great!" he shouted.

"Quiet, or she'll hear you."

"Is that really you, Katrina?" he whispered.

"Yes, James."

"Thank God you called. I've been worrying all night that I'd never see you again. Did your father give you a hard time?" The words came out in a rush.

"James, calm down, I'll tell you later. I love you with all my heart. Now tell me, love, where shall we meet?"

The reply had shaken him rigid. 'Her Love'! He felt elated.

"Now, Katrina, as soon as possible, I love you too."

They talked on the phone for a few minutes, trying to sort out where they should go, at least for the afternoon.

The Range Rover was parked close against the hedgerow bank, and although in the narrow road, it was completely camouflaged from the valley below. Rodrick stretched his arms as he looked intently towards the cluster of houses below, and the one in particular that he had been watching for the last two hours. Four times he had started the engine with the intention of driving the short distance to her home, then his nerve had failed, and he blamed it all on her brother. Without Richard to counsel or protect her, he could have confronted Katrina and got at the truth, knowing that her mother supported him wholeheartedly, and there would have been some support from George too.

Savagely, he beat the dashboard with his fist. How could she do this to him? Everyone at the stables was laughing behind his back. They all knew that she had deceived him: bitch, slag—the words rolled off his tongue as he looked through the misted glass. Then he saw the smears of red from his skinned knuckles, then sucked and tasted the raw blood oozing through the damaged skin before biting deeply into his forefinger, as if to increase his self-inflicted pain as he watched and waited.

Katrina replaced the receiver, took one long look around the room, snatched her handbag from the chair, took out her car keys and sprinted for the front door. Already she had projected her thoughts into the future, envisaged James' arms holding her tight, so with unseeing eyes she had slammed the door and ran down the path towards her car. The male shape she encountered was similar, but it was the form of someone that she had managed to avoid. Now they were on a fast collision course within the confines of the garden. WHACK! The open-handed vicious smack across her face made her teeth rattle. The next one missed as she stumbled onto the lawn.

"Whore, bitch!"

Katrina saw that his face was distorted as he shouted abuse after her fleeing figure, but he had not followed, and as she drove away, her rear-view mirror revealing Rodrick shaking his fist at her, the last words she heard were, "I'm goin' to get you sooner than later."

The shock from the blow was greater than the pain, and it took over ten minutes before she could stop shaking completely. Only by focusing on her forthcoming meeting with her lover could the ugly incident with Rodrick be blanked out for the present.

James walked stiffly towards their meeting place, head down, deep in thought: how could he compete with rich rival suitors?

From the driving seat low-down, Katrina watched as he limped towards her, then she smiled inwardly—the morning's work-out seemed to have taken its toll.

Looking up, he saw her waiting: the MG must have flown down the motorway in order to park before he got there. Grinning broadly, he went around the side of the car to greet her. The ridge running down his face was highlighted by the sun, and the dark around the eye seemed to shine and reflect its rays. Before the object of his affection was reached, Katrina was out of the car, and two soft hands held his face.

"What have they done to you, my love?" Then she

kissed him, not in passion but with the gentle touch of lips on a flower.

"It's nothing, doesn't hurt at all," he lied.

Then her arms slipped down around his waist and pulled his body into hers, and the pain in his side throbbed but was stifled by the beating of his heart. Within seconds she felt his breath on her neck grow hot, and a flush came into her cheeks. Then she felt his body grow taut, and knew it was time to pull away.

"James, where do you want to go?"

Walking to meet her, he had not given any thought as to where they would go, but his face betrayed his feelings and desires. Katrina looked at him and felt overwhelmed. She knew exactly what he was thinking, but with pressure from her mother and father to be home early so that she could prepare for the event, and with Rodrick lurking in the background, she felt more at ease away from the village.

She smiled. "Would you show me around Bristol down by the docks? They say it is very nice by the water."

"Great," was all he said, and although she watched carefully he seemed neither disappointed nor happy at her suggestion. The short drive down the M32 into the centre of the city passed by without incident. Although she watched the rear view mirror discreetly, nothing revealed itself to alarm her.

Katrina knew that if they had been travelling away from the built-up areas into the hills and vales of the country, James would have already made a move towards her, but, with her asking directions frequently, his thoughts were firmly on her driving. They parked the car, and walked idly hand in hand, looking into the windows of the department stores. There was nowhere here that his passion could be quenched, so she felt completely at ease—walking as a pair like any other anonymous couple out on this beautiful afternoon.

"Are you rich, Katrina?" James asked. It was not the right thing to say, but ever since his father had jibed at him about how much land her family owned, it had stuck at the back of his thoughts. Now he felt that he had known her forever, so the question had just come out naturally.

Katrina answered without any hesitation, "Not personally, I will inherit a fairly large sum when I'm twenty-five, from a grandmother, but that's a long time yet."

"That huge horse you ride, is he yours?"

"Yes, Father purchased him in Ireland for my sixteenth birthday."

"Why all the questions?" She looked at him quizzically with a slight frown on her face.

He laughed light-heartily. "Nothing really, it's only that my father said that Kelly is worth a lot of money, is he?"

"Have a guess?"

"I wouldn't have a clue."

"Go on." She poked him in the ribs which made him jump. Seeing his reaction and knowing that she had touched a sore spot which hurt, her arm was quick to hold him close. "Shall I kiss it better?"

"Wish you would, Katrina, but we might get arrested, then what would your father say?"

He was only joking but a small frown fleetingly darkened her face. James saw the change of expression—what a fool! The most important question had not been asked.

"Katrina, how was it with your family last evening?"

She smiled; it all seemed so long ago. "Fine. I told them that our relationship is only platonic, you are just a friend."

James had stopped to make sure he was hearing right. Had it fallen apart already? Was this the reason they were in the town, with buildings and people.

"Katrina, why did you say those things, why are you doing this to me?"

His legs felt that as if they had been kicked from under him, and in that one short sentence his aches and pain came back.

She saw the hurt look, then she turned so that they faced each other, and her hands went out so that her fingers locked into each lapel on his jacket. Then the power came as she gripped tightly. So this was how a horse was held on a short rein to stop him bolting.

James felt the strength as he was almost lifted forward until her face was close to his.

"James, look into my eyes, look deeply. There is no one else but you." She took a deep breath. "Today I promised Mother that I would be home early, and that is exactly what will happen. Tomorrow—can you leave your car at home when you go training, so that we can go into Bath for lunch? My treat—then I have a few things to purchase for my brother's wedding." The grip tightened and he felt her knee slip inside his groin. Her face was flushed as she stared wide-eyed at him, and they were so tight and intertwined that it was an effort for her even to whisper.

James turned his ear to her lips to catch her lowering tone, so that when her words came out they could be deciphered correctly.

"After I have taken you home, drive to the valley, open the gate and go down the dirt track to where we met yesterday morning, park the car off the bridlepath out of sight, then wait for me."

Turning his head to face her, for he thought she had finished, he was astonished when Katrina started to shake him.

"Please listen." The tone was almost pleading, but there was a steely edge in the two words. "Tomorrow evening will be the last time we will meet for a while." She felt his body go stiff, so she carried on quickly. "For the next few days Kelly will need all my attention to get the best out of him at Badminton. When we meet tomorrow night you will make love to me surrounded by swards of bluebells, and primroses, a magic bed of flowers to lie on!"

James was bewildered; she loved him with such intensity that it was frightening, and the strength in her body more than matched his own. Yet the night before, so pliable and submissive under his hands, he felt weak at the knees thinking about her even in the middle of town. How he should, or could, wait until tomorrow evening was beyond his comprehension. Katrina let him go, then ran off a little way. Within seconds he had caught and hugged her close and her whole body just melted into his arms.

"Come on, James, how much?"

The purchase price of the horse had completely slipped his mind, but he would have a stab at it. "Five hundred pounds."

"No, come on, James, try again." She laughed, and he noticed her eyes were looking skyward.

"Seven then."

"I give in, you will probably tell me that someone gave him to your father."

She laughed. "Kelly cost four thousand guineas as a four-year-old. Now he's eight, and worth..." She hesitated. "I would not sell him at any price. By the way the MG was for my twentieth, six weeks ago, so you see I have everything. Richard my brother brings presents from foreign places, and Mother buys clothes for me, and as a member of the young England team, father has made sure there is good sponsorship for my eventing—and as you know Badminton starts this week."

The short, sharp speech came tumbling out, and each sentence was like a misplaced hand on a shower tap letting its cold water needles strike to the very heart. James looked at her in awe as she lay gently swaying in his arms, looking out over the water. What he was holding was a bundle of dynamite, and he felt her father was right to question who his daughter was going out with.

"James, what are you thinking?"

"I wish it was tomorrow now," and he meant it.

They played that afternoon and into the early evening. No one else mattered except the two of them, and they kissed and held each other for brief moments, and, if his passion heightened, she would pull away laughing and reaffirm her promise. Nothing marred their travels, no phoning home, no crises of conscience as to what may or might not happen, two lovers in perfect harmony pleased and happy to be together.

The green dart was parked in the same lay-by from where it had departed many hours before. Its hood was raised against the glare of head lamps penetrating the interior, as other arrows hurtled the short distance from the island under the motorway to the ever-changing traffic lights.

Both its occupants were recovering from another passionate embrace. "James, you must go or I will be late," she whispered without very much conviction. "Look, all the windows are steamed up."

Slowly and reluctantly he withdrew his hand from the darkness, where his fingers had felt the hotness of her skin.

Now he lay back reluctantly in his seat, sweating profusely as he watched his love rearrange her attire. Katrina felt a strange premonition as his gaze passed over her body for the last time. She had an overwhelming feeling that tomorrow was going to be too late.

"James, I will see you at the training ground, shall I drive you home now?"

"No it's only a short way," and he pointed in the general direction along the duel carriageway.

Katrina started the engine as her love scrambled out of the car unwillingly, and shut the door.

"James," she called with a note of urgency in her voice, sensing that he was going to walk away. "Are you not going to kiss me goodnight? Shame on you!"

There was no need for her plea as he had already moved around to her open window, and, as he bent his head towards her, Katrina spoke again.

"Wait, I have something for you." With two hands she opened her gold interwoven chain and placed it around his neck.

"Katrina, why have you given me this?"

"Richard, my brother gave it to me. Now I want you to wear it, and think of our love for each other. Bye, James, see you tomorrow." Then with a squeal of rubber she was gone.

He could still feel her smile and laughter from earlier, and it gave him a warm glow inside as he started to walk the half-mile towards his home. The dual carriageway had a central stone divide reinforced with a steel barrier on top. On one side of the four-lane highway was a cycle track and walkway, and on the other was a rough grassed area which James was picking his way along carefully. The traffic was fairly heavy for a Sunday evening, and although there was a gap in the central reservation to cross, he had decided to stay on the dirt track until he reached the bridge that crossed the river, where it was much narrower. One third of the way to his destination, the almost musical swish of tyres was interrupted by a thud. James stopped and looked behind, expecting to see a slight collision as an over-eager driver had inadvertently shunted into the boot of the car in front at the traffic lights. Instead, the next moment he found himself hurtling to his left as he dived away from the out-of-control Range Rover that had mounted the grass verge and was careering straight for him.

Rodrick swore profusely as he skidded back on to the road. Throughout the afternoon he had watched the couple, and as his anger mounted so his hatred had switched briefly from Katrina to the stranger. Now he had been foiled in his first attempt to dispose of his rival. Then he laughed out loud, a high maniacal scream almost. The Range Rover swayed as it was driven at high speed in pursuit of his other quarry, although he knew that if Katrina was in a hurry he would not catch her, for she'd had over four minutes' start. Rodrick surveyed the empty road as he raced down towards the deserted village, then he shouted as he saw her car, "There is always tomorrow, bitch, you or your fancy man can't hide from me. I shall be waiting."

James struggled to his feet, then dusted himself down, all the time looking to where the tail-lights had disappeared, as if the driver was going to reverse and apologise for his momentary loss of control. Then he checked the traffic, before running across to the central reservation, climbed over, pausing before making it to the other side in haste. "Bugger, that was close," he muttered as he took out a cigarette and lit the end without breaking his stride as he moved quickly onward.

"Betty, look, we have a pansy for a son, what's that around your neck? Where did you buy that? A car boot sale? Funny colour."

"Leave him alone, can I have a look, James?"

"You can take it off, if you like, Mother?"

Betty looked for the fastener. There was none, the chain was open and stiff, and weighed in her hand, twenty times as heavy as any one of hers.

"James, this is gold, how much did it cost you?"

"Nothing, Mother, Katrina gave it to me."

John spoke as if he did not believe his wife. "It looks more like brass to me," he muttered as he held out his hand to feel the weight. Lightly in his palm he held the chain. Its colour seemed to mock him, and ask the question, what am I? Then it came to him and he started. Twelve years he had been searching for coins, and except for two sovereigns, and a couple of plated rings, the only real gold he had found was a very small part of a Roman torque.

"Dad, give it back."

"Hang on a minute." With that he went out of the room to retrieve the small shoe box which held his best finds. Wrapped up in tissue in a plastic folder was what he sought. Carefully he unwrapped the object and placed it next to the chain. Then he came back into the room, and he was not smiling at all.

"Betty that girl must be bonkers? Do you know what this is? It's twenty-four-caret gold, it must be worth a fortune."

James sighed. Not another guessing game about how much something was worth. He had already made a fool of himself once that day regarding Kelly's purchase price. But this was personal.

Betty took the chain John was admiring and placed it close to her neck. For a brief moment she felt a pang of jealousy, then it was gone, for she knew in her heart that, whoever the young lady was, she must love her son a great deal.

"John, go out and make some tea."

"But we...some of us drink coffee!"

"Just go away and leave us alone."

James sat down apprehensively at the table with his mother sitting opposite. He was back at school with his teacher looking down at him from the podium at assembly.

"James ,your father and I have never interfered in what you do, or who you go out with..." Betty bit her lip and paused to collect her thoughts; there was so much to say and the words must ring true. "Do you really, really, know what you are getting into? James, think carefully, no one gives a gold chain worth maybe over a thousand pounds to someone they only like, it's deeper than that."

"Look, Mother, we only met yesterday, as you know.

The only thing I can tell you is that her horse is worth well over ten thousand pounds, that she has her own car, and lives in a large house. Oh! And she has been invited to participate in some big riding event, Chipping Sodbury...no, Badminton, that's it."

Betty watched the tense expression on his face, but she made no comment when he lit up a cigarette, although in the house smoking was banned. James realised what he had done and laughed loudly, but it was a sound born of desperation not joy.

"Just treat her with respect, that's all I ask, then she will respect you. That's how you build a good relationship that will last." Betty took a deep breath. "Now go and let your father in, before the tea gets cold."

Walking into the kitchen he pondered on the words from his mother, then grimaced. If only she knew.

"James, are you seeing Katrina tomorrow?"

"Yes, Mother, we are going shopping in Bath, clothes for her brother's wedding."

Katrina was right. As he stroked the gold surface of the chain it seemed to soften, so that its texture felt like the soft strands of her hair sliding through his fingers. Long before the last reveller had left the bar, he was drawn into the half-sleep of the dreamer where all things are possible. As the spring moon cast a silvery beam across the valley it ever so briefly highlighted his love, and its net drew her to him so they were one.

Monday dawned with the threat of rain. The forecast for the day give an eight per cent chance of showers before dusk. Katrina looked at the radio alarm clock by the side of her bed, five to seven it showed. Normally with one bound she would have been out from under the covers and in the bathroom, before the radio burst into life in five minutes' time. Today, there was no need to hurry. Kelly would only need a small gentle hack to keep him calm; it was more for her benefit than his—there was no doubt that he was as fit as he could ever be. Then the rain came, not drizzle but a sharp spatter on the window as a gust of wind drove it against the house. The showers would help soften the ground which had grown hard over the last two weeks of clear blue skies and constant sun. Turning over and putting out a hand to forestall the music, she felt a slight pain, and her hand went to it—both her breasts were rock solid and seemed at the very least an inch larger. James! Out of bed she jumped and opened the wardrobe door so that the reflective mirror would give her a full profile. The discarded night-gown lay in a crumpled heap around her feet. Slowly she turned to catch the fleeting light from the window. If his hands made her grow like this in two days what would they look like in a year? She shuddered.

Kelly was difficult to handle this morning. The rain had come during darkness and was trying to work its way into the hard ground. Grass, flowers and trees drew in the life water, and gave out a sweet smell in appreciation of its coming. As the scent wafted around the valley the wild stallion in him surfaced with this rebirth of nature. Katrina had given him his head; both knew every inch of the ground where they trained over the years, but she held him perfectly under her control. Now they were trotting up the slope to the stable yard. Only one person was there, leaning on a broom waiting for her to pull up.

Mary Joe watched the mud-spattered rider dismount with worship in her eyes. To her, Katrina was all that epitomised eventing in this country, and one day she hoped that it would be her fortune to represent her own.

Katrina liked the South Carolina girl a lot; nothing was too much bother for her. Mucking out the stables, rubbing down the horses were all part of her chores. Always cheery and bright, her whole attitude brought her many mounts to ride and train in the weeks when their owners were away.

The stable owner had always ridden Kelly for her

if she was away, but now she knew that the American girl was more than capable if he was not available. Her apprenticeship was nearly over, if you could call it that, and Katrina knew that in the not-very-distance future Mary Joe could well be competing against her in the arena.

"Alan has asked why you are not taking Kelly across to Badminton today. I told him that you wanted to keep him here as long as possible, was that all right?"

Katrina gave almost a secret smile before replying; horses were already moving into the stables just a few miles away, but she had phoned and cancelled Kelly's departure until the next morning. This decision was a completely selfish gesture on her part. The reason was that later that evening she would take the stallion down and introduce him to her other love. Tethered nearby, he would watch over them, so that if anyone intruded within a radius of fifty metres Kelly would let her know.

"Remember what you promised, Mary Joe."

The girl smiled sheepishly. "How is James?"

"Fine, he is just fi..." Her words dried up as a large cloud covered the sun, sending a dark shadow across the yard, which made her shiver.

They were both laughing out loud, as Alan came towards them from the farm house.

"You two are happy, can I join in?"

Katrina smiled at her thoughts. If her mother knew what was going around in her head at this moment she would have had a fit—it was so frivolous, but to her it was important. Then she made a decision—two-piece bikini as small as possible, or what if she could tan all over?

James had a much easier morning than he had anticipated; all of the first-team professionals were on the field broken up into groups, with their own exercises to perform. The most striking aspect of their activity that James noticed was the shouting.

James dived and punched the ball from the heads of the opposing forwards and it did not matter how they tried, they could not score. Highly elated, he walked into the dressing room to change, looked at his reflection in the mirror, and came back to earth with a bump. The injury was a mixture of bright scarlet and blue, although there was no pain. To the casual observer it looked like a baseball bat had made close contact with his face. Carefully he dressed, all the time watching the other players and the trainer. As much as he wanted to flee, the words had stuck—you are part of a squad not a loner, he reminded himself. So now he was impatiently waiting for a few to leave.

At last he made for the dressing-room door, and made his exit as the trainer smiled to himself, for he had watched the keeper dress, then undress again. Glancing out onto the car park, he saw the reason for the haste—the girl was waiting and he knew that he would have hurried too.

"Oh my God!" He nearly dropped his holdall, for Katrina was standing with her back to the MG with her hands draped like the models on the advertisements. She was dressed in a skimpy one-piece mini-skirt outfit. Every contour of her body was highlighted by the figure-hugging material, and it left nothing to the imagination—what you saw, you got.

Later that morning when she had left the stables to get changed, and had tried to decide what to wear for her meeting with her love, she had toyed with what had been discarded twice before—always some excuse for not wearing them but that had changed now; she had a plan.

Catherine waved goodbye as her daughter went out of the gate. Nothing seemed amiss—just a new sweater and jeans, although she could not remember when they had bought them.

Half a mile away she had stopped, and within a minute off had come the wide-bottom trousers and an image transformation took place. Richard's birthday money had bought the outfit. Although it had been very expensive, as soon as her hands smoothed the material down around her thighs and she saw it was wrinkle-free, she knew that it had been more than worth the money paid.

Players whistled as they came into the car park, but when her man closed on her they shut up—six foot plus, with half a black eye and a red and purple ridge, he looked mean to say the least. Grinning broadly, he closed on her quickly, and made full bodily contact. He felt her start as he lifted her easily onto the car bonnet away from him. In that moment of closeness the flimsy material was no barrier to his physical desires, and then she knew that her choice had been right.

"You are a dream, Katrina."

"Get me down, you big bully, you look like a pirate."

James slowly let her body slide down so that he could enjoy every part of her. When at last her feet touched the concrete, and she had felt her skirt rise inches higher, she knew and felt the passion within his taut body, knew that both of them would hardly make the evening.

"Lucky sod," someone shouted, while others blew their car horns.

"Come on, Katrina, let's get out of here."

"Where shall we go first, James? We have plenty of time."

One look from him was enough to give more than a direct answer.

"No, not till later."

"But I haven't said a word."

"You don't have to—so where would you like to go?"

Then he had a vision of her long brown legs stretched out in front of him and the secret dark place between, and his stomach turned over in anticipation.

"On the river. I'd like to go for a row. Is that all right with you, Katrina?" More blasts on the horns.

They both sat in the car, and as the seat belts were adjusted and his eyes never wandered from her legs, she knew the power of thought and laughed so that he looked at her with eyes wide. And, unbeknown to him, she patted the rolled-up bundle beside her.

James never even asked if on the river you could hire boats, but Katrina seemed to know where to drive. The sun was out and it was warm in the car and so was he and the more they drove the hotter he got. Katrina worked the pedals and as she did the skirt seemed to move higher and higher, beckoning him on. Now she had upped the temperature with what she was wearing, how was he to know that the cake was for viewing only, not eating whole. Click went his seat belt as he cleared the obstacles that could hinder his movement.

Katrina had been driving carefully, watching the back of the car through the mirror, so that if anyone came close they could pass. When he had held her tight and she had felt his physical hardness boring into her, she knew that what came next would not be just playing around, he would go for it in a big way, whatever the time of day. Katrina spun the wheel and the car veered across the road and into an open field gate opposite. Stopping quickly, she opened the door and got out. Before he could recover his breath after the fright he'd received, he saw she was standing with her hands on hips, looking at him.

"Not now, please."

James got out of the car and took some deep breaths, then a few more and he felt the tension ease. Slowly he walked towards her, took her hands in his and kissed her lightly on the forehead. Katrina did not respond with hungry lips. Instead, she just stood silent as the breeze ruffled their hair, for he had called a truce, at least for the moment.

In the distance he saw the park where they had met a short time ago.

" Katrina, could we drive into the park, and walk from there? I need some fresh air."

"James, that's the best idea you've had this morning."

They wandered on, watching the squirrels dart along the ground, then scramble up the trees, and paused for a few moments to watch their movements and daring.

"James, are you hungry?"

He looked at her and she knew he was.

"I know, we'll go in the Pump Room for a meal, is that all right?"

James shrugged his shoulders. Any name in Bath was new to him; it sounded imposing and he felt the five ten-pound notes in his pocket and wondered.

Katrina saw the look. "This is my treat, it is our last day together for ages, anyway, you're a visitor."

"What do you mean, our last day, Katrina?"

They were still in the park but she would not have cared where they were, as she apologised with a kiss laced with passion. "I hope you will come to the event when I ride, but there will be lots to do and thousands of people around us. That's why it's our last day together, I told you last evening."

The restaurant was pleasantly cool as they walked into its interior. To James it was impressive with its marble statues in the hall, and when they were taken to their table by a waitress he felt great.

Katrina was all chatter, and it was obvious that she had been to this place many times before. The imposing menu was brought and placed on the spotless white tablecloth.

"Where is the music coming from?" he whispered.

"Over there—they call it chamber music. Nice, do you like it?"

James grinned. "Excellent, shall we order?"

The meal was to a high standard, and when they had finished he praised it and meant it.

Katrina knew she had made a mistake, for as soon as they had walked out of the restaurant he was all over her like a rash; as for her trousers, they were a mile away in the car. Surely he would not try anything in a rowing boat?

"Katrina?"

"Yes," she replied meekly as his arm held her tight against him. They were on the bank queuing for a rowing skiff with two other couples. Four boats came in together, its occupants all laughing as they commented on each other's rowing. She noticed that the females in the party wore either slacks or jeans. Katrina stepped into the boat gingerly as her ardent love held the skiff firm. Sitting down was not going to be particularly easy, especially as, for some reason, most of the men who had just disembarked suddenly decided to moved closer. Holding tightly on to the hem of the high-riding material, she managed to sit down, close her knees and wrap her legs sideways under the seat. Then she shut her eyes and cursed that her modesty cover was still in the car. Some of the more seasoned rowers wore shorts for comfort and skimmed past them easily, but James knew that with the strength in his arms he could just row and row forever. Katrina began to relax as she watched the strength flowing through her love sitting opposite—he was fully occupied in guiding them away from other incoming craft. Ten minutes later with clear water around them, he shipped the oars and let the boat drift towards the bank out of the main stream, where he removed his shirt.

Katrina gasped as she saw the surface damage to his sides from the constant contact with the ground, and the number of stud marks on his body from mistimed flailing boots. He could not have planned it more perfectly, for as she sat up and moved forward on the seat, her legs opened like the wings of a butterfly, and the whiteness of her thighs above the stocking tops made him gulp. Katrina saw the crimson flush but did not care. Kneeling close to him, she placed her arms around his waist, laid her head on his chest and held him tight. All her maternal instincts had been aroused and she wanted desperately to protect him.

"Lucky sod," someone shouted and he could have sworn it was the same voice he had heard at the training ground. Softly she spoke to him of her deepest love, and then he to her, and as his heartbeat slowed down she moved back. But this time his eyes never left hers for he had seen the wings of fire and was satisfied that they would not fly away, but would be folded for only a short time.

Wandering around shops was an alien activity to him, but with his love dragging him along by the hand and her enthusiasm for him to give an opinion on anything ranging from a pair of shoes to a figure-hugging sweater, he soon got into the mood. There was always the added bonus of a slightly open curtain, but some shop assistant always seemed to be watching, so that he would avert his eyes reluctantly and look at nothing in particular. Katrina squeezed his hand as they walked towards what she wanted to show him, although she could see that he was embarrassed as the small pieces were held up to her figure. She smiled in triumph as he picked what she had already set her heart on. Again his hand moved up to his neck to feel her gift from the night before, while into her bag went another purchase.

"James, my love, why do you keep touching the chain?" They had stopped and she was very near to him. "Has the sun on the river made you sore? Let me see."

He grinned and pulled her to him. "If I tell you, I want you to promise not to make fun of me."

"I won't, cross my heart, tell me," she pleaded.

"Well?" He paused. "You won't laugh?"

She nodded her head vigorously.

"You remember when we were looking for the names of any of our ancestors in the abbey, and you wandered off—well, if I stroked the chain you came back to me almost at once. Are you laughing?"

She shook her head again.

"When you gave me the chain you told me I would think of you. Well every time you have bought an item for your trip to Barbados, I touch it so that you will come back to me."

The words as they came out were strong with conviction and meaning, and as she looked up at her handsome lover-to-be, she felt just a glazing of water misting her eyes, and for the first she did not want to go to her brother's wedding. For certain, her love was experiencing the same feelings she had felt on many occasions when out of the jewel box the interwoven rope had come as if it had told her to wear the band around her neck. Richard had never said that he had bought the object or where it had come from. There had been no special occasion like Christmas or a birthday. He had just turned up one day five years ago; placed it round her neck, told her he loved her like he always did, then vanished. That was strange, as when she had run down the stairs to show her mother what he had given her, she had said, "Richard? I haven't seen him."

Before driving away the other night some impulse or force had made her stop and place her treasure around his neck. No, she would not laugh, but now she was older it was time to ask her brother how the gold necklace was obtained.

A chilly wind blew in short gusts as they made their way more quickly back to the MG, making it colder than when they had left it hours before. Pulling into the warmth of his body she made no protest when every now and again his hand closed around her breast. There were no buttons for him to explore further so they made the car in good time. Quickly, she changed into the wide-bottom jeans. She saw his face almost drop as he watched her in silence but her mind was made up. There was no way that she could drive with his hand exploring her inner thighs—it would be just too much for her to handle.

The time was only four-thirty as they powered up the hill on the Stroud road out of Bath, and he watched her work the gear lever and the accelerator as he had done before, then laughed out loud.

"What is it?"

"It's those jeans you're wearing; they must be the biggest passion-killers around." He pinched a piece of the material and shuddered.

"No they're not. I saw you looking at more than a few girls with these on while we were in Bath."

James had to admit that some of the shrink-wrapped type did look very tasty, but what Katrina was wearing—ugh! So he never answered her implied question.

Now they were nearing the Westerleigh road, which was narrow with high banks and hedgerows, and as it twisted its way down towards Downend there were a sprinkling of places to slack your thirst, if you were so inclined.

James was more than happy to consider one of them and was looking forward to a pint as he knew that only a mile or so down the hill was a very tidy place. Katrina tensed as the intersection approached. It was devoid of traffic, and without changing gear or speed she was on the slip road to the M4 in a flash. James sat bolt upright. So Katrina was taking him home early? Now there were no trees, no high hedgerows, just open fields stretching away in the distance and nowhere to get off.

"Katrina?" Her name came out with force.

She laughed inwardly, not at him, for her love was so overwhelming that she would gladly die to make him happy.

"You promised." It came out sulkily.

"And I always keep my promises. We will meet this evening where the hedgerow joins the track. You can drive your car close to our rendezvous."

For a moment she glanced at his face and as she did so all became clear.

"But first we're going to a pub—highly recommended. It serves excellent beer, and has good company—the place where you left your mates yesterday...Unless you're ashamed of me?" She waited, hardly breathing, for his reply.

"You are beautiful, and very, very clever."

"Katrina, you will take those baggy jeans off before we go in." The black number slipped out easily without a mark or crease showing, as the bell-bottoms disappeared under her seat.

"Same as usual, James, anything else?" the landlord asked.

"Dry white wine, please," Katrina whispered, although there was only a sprinkling of people in the lounge.

They both sat staring into space. There was so much to say, yet each knew that this evening, although momentous, would also be their last together for what seemed like ages.

"That's enough, no more wine, thank you."

Then he saw her look at the clock on the wall, and knew that the time was drawing close to their parting.

"James, how far do you live from here?"

"Just across the green, why?"

"This is a long way from the dual carriageway where we met the other day."

"Five minutes, well maybe ten at the most."

"I could have dropped you off outside if you had asked." Again the quick glance her watch, as James downed the last of his pint, then stood up. Katrina followed him out to the car park. There was no time for any lingering passionate kisses, the day was already drawing to a close. There could be no risk of riding Kelly in the twilight, so it was imperative that she left straightaway. James kissed her once softly, then watched her drive away into the distance. Turning away, he sprinted across the green to home.

Catherine watched her daughter alight from the MG in a hurry, and saw her face was flushed as she almost ran to the front door. Her entire demeanour seemed odd. The black leotard top was so tight that you could see the stitches on her brassiere underneath. It then disappeared into a pair of shapeless blue denim jeans which looked big enough for George to wear. Completing this ghastly outfit was a large buckled belt that looked like one of her brother's of leather army-type, and white plimsolls that were almost completely hidden in the bell-bottoms. Shutting her eyes, she visualised the pair of light lemon two-piece suits, with matching accessories, that took pride of place in the window of a shop in Bath—excellent material, for the climate in Barbados, at more than a fair price. Now her daughter was going hippie! It must be that new fellow, George said that he would be a bad influence on her. Katrina saw her mother watching from the window as she scrambled to fit the key in the lock, then it clicked and she was inside the door making for the stairs in haste.

"Katrina, dear, do you want anything to eat?" her mother called.

"Yes, Mother," was her instant reply.

Catherine wanted to call again from the kitchen, but the water was running into the bath so she busied herself making cheese and tomato sandwiches for them both.

The cowboy passion-killers as James called them were folded neatly for disposal in the refuse bin, the other garment that had nearly set him alight was scrunched into a small ball and hidden safely away in a drawer. Her one and only suspender belt disappeared into a Marks and Spencer carrier bag covered by her riding socks. It would be washed carefully quite soon as it was her intention to wear it often, with or without her mother's approval. Katrina hummed a tune as she swished the bath oil around, building large white mounds of bursting bubbles on the very hot water. Making a noise drowned out the sound of her heart beat, and slightly ease the tension that she felt building around her. At least, that was her theory as she gingerly eased her body into the scolding water. Laid out neatly on the bed were the clothes that she would wear in a very short time to her secret rendezvous. Brown stretch jodhpurs were her choice: although she favoured her light-coloured ones, these dark trousers would not show any grass stains so were more practical for what she planned. Katrina smiled. What a calculating witch she was! What if her parents were to know that if she discarded her woollen sweater and removed her trousers, she would be completely naked underneath with no pants or bra to hide her modesty? The water was more bearable now, so she lay back and let the heat and the steam penetrate every part of her body. When she climbed out of the bath glowing like a freshly cooked lobster, she would not only feel fantastic but would be completely fresh and wholesome.

James Justin Eagles hated the shower. It was not that the water came out in dribbles—on the contrary the perforated nozzle spurted needle darts in their thousands. The cubicle was much too small for his frame, and it was a work of art to adjust the water temperature from the outside without stepping into the small space provided.

The only advantage over the more conventional running of a bath was that it was quick, and as time was of primary importance he gone for the fastest. Now with soap in his eyes burning like fire, and the showerhead almost touching his scalp, and his arms scraping the sides, he wondered if he had not been too hasty in his choice. The car was already facing down the road—no opening the gates then reversing from the driveway. Everything was ready for a fast getaway, and every minute would count. One thing was for sure: he would not be late for this passionate encounter and all that it promised—when they would both erupt like a volcano in the blackness of the night.

The house was empty except for the dog, and there was not even enough time to make a fuss of her. James brushed his teeth vigorously with an ample supply of paste, so that it whisked around his lips making them taste of peppermint. Washing his mouth with copious amounts of water until he was sure that any white resin had disappeared, he then dabbed around his mouth with a damp towel, cleaning off any specks that marred his features.

"Ready!" he shouted, then punched the air in

excitement. Looking at his watch, he realised that only a short time had transpired since Katrina had departed for home. The M4 Motorway was crowded with traffic, so, as the Ford Escort powered along the side road that was almost deserted, the driver felt glad that this was the route that he had chosen. The sun had slowly disappeared from a cloudless sky, leaving a bright reddish horizon in the west, and the local weather forecast was good for the next couple of days, threatening only a slight chance of an odd shower this evening. Away to the right stood Home Farm, and as his father on a Saturday morning turned away to the left, so did James. He approached the village apprehensively; there was no doubt that he was early. At least he could drive along the track without using any lights to betray his presence in the valley.

Parked next to the sheep-shearing barn close against the wall stood a four-wheeled drive Land Rover, and horsebox. James stopped the car and looked across the fields for any sign of movement. Seeing none, he drove on slowly towards his destination. Katrina had been specific with her instructions, drawing a neat plan for him to follow, not knowing that he had already walked the route only a couple of days before looking for her home. James wondered whether his love had left the first gate, the one that barred the entrance to the valley, open purposely. At least there was no delay; within seconds the car was bumping along the hard track away from human habitation, and, most important, prying eyes.

Katrina (Anne, after her great aunt), began to panic.

Everything had slotted into place so neatly until she had joined her mother in the kitchen. That had been a disaster. Soon the questions were coming thick and fast; just small talk, but she knew that her father would arrive before long and it would start all over again—Richard's wedding and all that it entailed, like when could they go shopping in Bath for their clothes. A close second came the horse trials, why was Kelly still at Home Farm? There was no mention of the greatest and the most important aspect of her life, James.

"I think it's going to rain; look at those black clouds gathering, dear. There's no need to go out. Alan will phone if there is even the slightest problem at the stable."

"Mother, I must go, Mary Joe will be waiting." That was true but not in the sense that her mother believed.

"Stay for a few more minutes until your father returns. Both of us together should talk him into having tomorrow or Wednesday morning off." Catherine waited for a reply. When one was not forthcoming she turned away from the window and found that her daughter had vanished.

Katrina took the long route to the farm. Her love would be somewhere close by, and her father too. Either one would wonder where she was going if they met her on the road. James would have had a fit if suddenly she were to blast past him going in the opposite direction. She smiled triumphantly; at least she had been clever enough to open the gate for him earlier, on the way home. Six minutes later, holding her breath with excitement, Katrina very slowly inched her transport across the steel cattle grid, trying not to betray her presence. Then with its engine dead, the car rolled smoothly towards the waiting figures at the bottom of the slope.

"Everything all right, Mary Joe?" Katrina asked anxiously.

"Yep, no problem at all." Even if there had been she would not have admitted it.

"Katy, where are you taking Kelly? Surely you are not going out training in this half-light?"

When the phone call had come for her to saddle up the horse, what time it was had not registered at first. Now with the light fading fast she was really worried.

"If I tell you what is happening, will you promise not to give my secret away to anyone?" Katrina wanted to confide in the girl. Her mother or father were not remotely interested in the fact that a stranger had completely stolen her from them, and everything that she had held in high esteem before had now crumbled into nothing, now that she was totally besotted, in love.

"Promise, I promise," the South Carolina girl trilled and so loudly echoed the sound that Katrina cringed. She was sure that every one within half a mile would have heard the American's voice.

"You know how much I love Kelly?"

The girl nodded vigorously, before adding, "So do I."

"Well…" Trying to find the right words was difficult. How could she say that sexual intercourse in the woods was part of her plan? Should she confide her innermost secrets or thoughts? At least with Mary Joe helping at

Badminton, there could be a possibility of slipping away for a short time without her father or mother knowing. It would not break her promise—just an hour or two alone together each day would cheer him up no end, and her too for that matter.

"Katy, you were going to tell." The voice was desperate.

Far down the valley from where the sun's rays had disappeared over an hour ago, the evening shadows had merged the trees and bushes into a single mass. Close against a hedge half-hidden from the bridlepath a car was parked; standing on its bonnet stood the figure of a man. James peered from the gloom towards the much higher and rapidly darkening westerly rim. Ten minutes ago the sky was clear and bright, now black clouds were moving across from the south and he heard more than felt the first spots of rain. Three hundred and fifty metres closer to Home Farm, halfway down one side of the slope, and blending into the trees, stood the bay gelding. For the last half an hour it had not moved as its rider repeatedly scanned the landscape looking for any movement. The hidden watcher had observed the driver's actions and knew that within a very short time someone would join him. Now a blind rage was building rapidly as he waited impatiently. They were whispering behind his back and sniggering at the stable yard, and it was all her doing. Yes, four years ago the accident had happened, which had given her that prominent scar.

That had been inflicted for pushing him into second place. How could he repay her for humiliating him in front of the other horse riders? Badminton, that was the key—the most important thing that she had ever wanted was to receive an invitation to ride at this, the world's greatest four-day event. Now that she had, it was his duty to take it away. Across the fields the distinct tone of the small sports car had alerted him, and he listened intently until the unmistakable rattle of the cattle grid sounded. Now he knew exactly where his quarry was driving to. Simple was the plan, and as he drooled over its ingenuity with his warped mind, a wolfish grin spread across his face. Maybe there was a possibility that with his cunning both of them would pay. Katrina would walk down the bridlepath unaware of his presence. As soon as her figure came in sight he would charge from the copse and ride right through her shouting that his horse had bolted. Estimated injuries—a couple of broken ribs, perhaps an arm as well. With the sixteen hands' Arab out of control her new boyfriend, if he wanted to be a hero, would get some of the same—the outcome just an *unfortunate accident.* Sneering as anger boiled over him like a tidal wave, then grinning as he gloated at the dreamed-of retribution for all the wrongs that had been heaped upon him, his emotions stretched his body like a piano wire, the tenseness within him making the horse become uneasy and restless. Every few minutes he would finger the short leather whip tucked in his boot. If she rode her stallion down, and he hoped she would, just think of the pain that he could inflict. Wetting his lips, he grimaced. Every thought of an accident was slowly disappearing, now the only possible outcome was his total revenge.

Mary Joe could see that although her heroine was a great horse rider where every move seemed to come naturally, Katy was clearly finding great difficulty in describing the affairs of her heart. "Shall I walk with you to the road?"

The rider was grateful that the uneasy silence, although it lasted for only half a minute, was broken. "Fine, that will be fine." The stock words tumbled from her lips as the three of them including Kelly who walked on the grass so as not to betray their presence, moved swiftly towards the open-gated entrance

"James is waiting, and this is our watchdog, should anyone come near."

The horse snorted as if he knew what his mistress was saying. Both laughed at his intrusion.

"There you are, I told you."

They were now well away from the farm, so that Katrina could speak almost normally, not that her hidden beating heart was anywhere near that state. Within a few minutes his arms would encircle her, and their moist warm lips would devour each other, and his hands… . She shuddered as a large droplet of water from a hanging branch drove into her soft hot skin, and rolled like a miniature waterfall from her neck to her navel. Mary Joe sensed the mood-swing now that they had reached the tarmac road. Without a word she hugged Katy fiercely so that their cheeks pressed tightly together.

The Californian felt a faint pang of jealousy. What price would she pay to ride down into the Valley of Dreams, if Her Love could miraculously appear from thousands of miles away?

Kelly gave them a hard nudge as if to say, come on, I am here too. Katrina pulled away from the now loosened grasp, steadied the horse, and mounted quickly. Without a word the American ran across the road and opened the gate, then watched fascinated as her true friend, head held high, slowly trotted past.

Storm clouds that had built into a towering mass stretching away to the west seemed to be retreating, leaving to the east a clear, bright sky, with a fresh spring moon casting a white light. There seemed almost a clean split in the sky that followed the bare whitish path that they had taken. Within seconds the horse tried to pick up his stride, but she held him firmly in check. Kelly snorted, almost as if he was protesting. Katrina leaned forward on his neck and whispered, "Quiet, we must surprise him." Although sound seemed to travel further at night she knew that her love would not have heard the noise, not the distance he was from them at this moment.

The dark rider felt the bay gelding stiffen, then saw its ears prick, and knew for certain that what he had been waiting for was coming.

James felt uneasy; the sounds around him in the grass and bushes were completely alien to him. Five times in the last few minutes he had heard rustlings that made his nerves tingle. The moon had broken from the cloud cover and sent a soft silvery sheen, increasing the brightness of the open spaces but deepening the shadows. Then he grinned—there was no need to have been early and wait almost three-quarters of an hour, but it had been his choice, and he was brave and strong. Nothing would frighten him.

Then the pitiful scream came, bouncing off the sides of the valley to pierce his eardrums, and hammer into his brain so that the hair on the back of his neck stood up in shock. James started to run like he had never ran before. Desperation drove him forward as the anguished cries for help echoed amongst the trees.

Mary Joe was leaning on the wooden gate staring into space, dreaming of olden days with knights in shining armour, and how her Katy (Guinevere) was now riding forth into the night for a secret meeting with her lover Lancelot. Ten minutes had passed since the portcullis had been opened and her lady had ridden out, and she sighed as her fingers moved around the rim of the discarded hard hat, as though it was a crown worn by her queen.

Funnelled between the sloping walls and carried on the wind came the cry, then another. Without any hesitation the girl began to move fast towards the farm. Alan jumped with fright as the door to the living room burst open, and a distorted red-faced figure, gasping for breath, blurted out, "Kat—y's in tr—ouble, d—own t—he v—alley, at—tack—ed," then wrenched violently and was sick in the hearth.

Even for him who was used to the accent, the words were almost indecipherable, but her actions spelt trouble.

Quickly he unlocked the gun cabinet, grabbed a twelve-bore shotgun, then with a handful of cartridges disappeared out of the door. The bearer of the news tried to follow, but was much too late as the four-wheel drive Land Rover rocketed out of the stable yard.

Katrina watched the landscape out in front change from a gloomy grey into a silvery dusty white as the moon broke from the cloud cover. Glints of light sparkled in the darkness as its rays passing over like a torch, reflected briefly on the car's glass windows. Three hundred and fifty metres at the most was her estimation.

Although James was still invisible against the dark undergrowth, she knew that within minutes they would be united. Kelly tried to pick up the pace, but she held him firmly in her grasp; there was no obstacle that could harm either of them. Although as a professional she would have condemned any other rider of her class as being completely stupid for even taking the slightest risk, Katrina had fought a long and hard battle with her inner self even to contemplate the action that she was taking. But her heart had won the day, and now she was nearing her lover.

The sharp clipping of his hoofs on the path would soon alert her waiting lover, if he had not spotted their dark outline against the lightness of the sky. Eyes firmly focused in front for the first sighting, she tensed, wanting so desperately the first kiss, to hug and to hold. The horse slowed and she knew that he had seen him. "Whoa, whoa." The words were of encouragement, soft and gentle, as Kelly veered off the path to the right.

9

The pain across her back came so suddenly and with such fierceness, that all her breath seemed to leave her body in a gust. Shortened rawhide bullwhip lashed out again, cutting deep around her forehead and splitting the old white scar tissue asunder so that blood cascaded into her eyes. Then she screamed and screamed, as it lashed her unmercifully. She drove her knees into Kelly, but through red blood-spattered eyes she saw that his reins were held firm by the other rider, who grunted and swore with each swish of the whip. Katrina tried to protect her face from the biting leather thong, as they went round and round the circle of pain. All her senses blurred into a dull shock under the relentless strokes. Now completely blind, no sound came from her lips as she was yanked from her horse and sent crashing to the ground. Rodrick laughed, an insane sound, as he surveyed the crumpled heap close to the horse's hoofs. Now he would finish her for good. Badminton! He laughed again.

Kelly had smelt the blood and heard the cries of his mistress but the skilful rider had held him tight. Now his captor was bending forward, untangling the leather reins which in the struggle had twisted around his wrist. The soaking wet leather whip tightened in his hand as a black shadow came between the two horses, but he had been waiting. Lashing at the unprotected head and shoulders like a skilled lancer with a cutlass, he laughed maniacally into the night sky, but no sound came from his victim. Kelly bit hard into the bay who reared in fright, and as its hoofs struck the ground its rider momentarily lost his position. Two large hands pulled him down from the saddle as a hard head drove into the bridge of his nose. Rodrick felt the agony as it shattered, and screamed in pain as he was lifted bodily into the air and threw onto the hard path. James heard the crack as a bone broke and knew that his love's attacker would not bother either of them for some time. And if he tried? There was so much anger in him for vengeance that he could kill now without any remorse. Yet, as Katrina lay moaning, curled up in a ball, his thoughts were for her alone.

Dark was the trampled ground that bore the scarred body, made darker by the wet red specks of blood mingled with wool from her maroon jumper, now shredded and scattered about. James touched her cautiously and tenderly, although every instinct told him to hug her tight and the nightmare would disappear. Wild thoughts were rushing through his brain; how could he attract attention? Should he carry his love to the car, or drive the car to her? The latter idea was discarded; with the maniac still alive he would not leave her for one minute. All the time he was hovering over her, wanting to touch but scared that it would give her more pain, and as the seconds ticked by he felt more panic. Then he felt the sticky residue on his fingers. What if she bleed to death without him doing anything for her; how could he live with that for the rest of his life? Crack went a dry stick under his foot. Fire—light a fire; the thought slotted into place neatly, but a deeper darker secret thought urged him to kill her tormentor, and then run to his car and drive for help in the village.

Scrabbling on his knees in the dark undergrowth, relying on instinct and ignoring the pain, he quickly pulled handfuls of dry tinder from the hedges and grass. "Please, please, let someone spot the flames," he shouted, as the lighter flint clicked, and the small spark took hold to send a sheet of light into the blackness. Ripping off his shirt he went as if to place it on the fire, then changed his mind, turned and moved towards the curled-up figure on the ground. Gently he placed the open garment over her back to hide the congealing mess of stripes angled in random pattern across her. Five minutes only would he give, then he would become the hunter. His adversary lay just outside the circle of light given off by the fire. James could not see the broken leg but knew from experience the tell-tale sound emitted as he had struck the ground. The discarded weapon of torture lay black and evil and bore into his sight. Picking it from the ground he went to toss it into the flames, changed his mind, and walked out of the light towards its former owner. No one was there yet Katrina lay only a few yards away.

Had he been wrong? Was the rider not injured, and instead just waiting for him to leave her unprotected and finish what he had started? Blue light from the moon had vanished as the cloud gained ascendancy over the landscape, and out in the darkness he heard the scraping of hoofs on the hard soil, then a voice urging its passage. Holding the whip tightly, James began to run towards the sound, then stopped as two headlamps not more than half a mile away pierced the night, sending long searchlight beams along the valley floor.

Alan had seen the fiery beacon from a distance. At least this was the spot; whoever had built the fire had some sense. He shuddered as an awful thought came into his head. Leaning across he pulled the gun closer. What if someone or something was on fire? Movement off to his left caught his eye; the hindquarters of the bay gelding disappearing into the gully. What he failed to see was its owner hanging on grimly as the horse dragged him away from immediate danger.

James stood in the middle of the track waiting, and was surprised when the Land Rover stopped at least twenty yards away.

From the Land Rover, bright beams of light played over the bare chest of the figure holding the bull-whip, and as the driver drew nearer dark smears of blood stood out clearly on the torso of whoever it was. Alan felt sick: it was almost like a film set with Indiana Jones standing in his path, but this was for real, and far more serious. Two cartridges were claimed from his jacket pocket, slipped into the breach, and with a quick movement without once taking his eyes off the standing figure, the deadly steel blue barrels were loaded. Opening the door cautiously, and holding the twelve-bore pointing downwards he moved slowly towards the now urgently gesturing nightmare.

"Tony, is that you?" he called without much conviction. Every one knew that Katrina was meeting the fellow from Bristol. It was his idea that had drawn them together in the first place. Where was Katrina? Mary Joe had definitely said "attack". As he moved closer so the gun barrels moved higher without Alan even noticing the subtle change.

"James, you know, Alan? From Bristol. Katrina's been hurt, we must get her to hospital quickly. Look, she's lying over here."

The words were shouted with some urgency as the speaker realised that two dark menacing holes were pointing directly at his chest. From the darkness came a moan as if to emphasise the point. Alan dropped the gun barrels and ran across to where he was pointing. "Who attacked her, did you see?"

"I don't know who it was. Katrina was meeting me further down the valley, I heard her scream and ran, but she was too far away, the rider was lashing her with this whip when I arrived."

"Would you know him again?"

"Alan, please, no more questions, drive and get help

quickly, I don't even know the name of this valley, let alone where we are in it."

The driver nodded in agreement. The instructions made sense; funny thing was he had not mentioned how her attacker had been driven off, and whether there was a possibility that he would return.

"I will stay with..." James felt his stomach knot, and the bitter-sweet taste of bile washed around his mouth. One wave as the Land Rover lurched crazily past, then he was violently sick. Cold and bleak was the night now that their togetherness had been trampled into the dust. He shivered and automatically fed the fire so that the heat radiated warmth into the huddled shape. Moving across, he lay down close, and then ever so gently worked his hand under her neck.

Katrina was riding the pain barrier of hell. Her dark brown stallion had changed to jet black, and its nostrils flared as they smashed through the trees. Thorns pierced her body, and branches scored her face, thundering hoofs drove out the wildlife from their secret places to be trampled under foot. Bursting out into the open from the wood, the horse galloped on. The pain was still with her, but the way ahead was clearly marked. Away to the right lay the impressive Badminton house. "No, no."

James froze; those were definite words from her lips, and there were more signs of movement but of no particular pattern.

Searing leather-burnt hands strove desperately to halt the pounding hoofs, but to no avail. Onward it moved relentlessly towards its goal.

Two shotgun blasts echoed across the top of the trees, sending the nesting rooks whirling and protesting into the night sky. The half-naked protector paused from feeding the fire as the noise rolled down into the valley. What if her attacker was coming back with a gun? He felt her startle as the sound vibrated around them, and moved closer so that his body could protect hers.

Katrina heard the sound and looked upward with unseeing eyes into the grey sky. The shattered bird slowly spiralled down, and as it descended towards the lake the crowd grew silent. Devil horse corkscrewed the fence as the dead pigeon dropped in front of his sights, but the pain-racked rider forced him upwards. Over they went locked together—another few inches and they would have cleared. Katrina felt Kelly's body change under her as his back legs straightened, caught by the wooden barrier. The two of them plunged downwards. Pivoted forward out of the saddle in seeming slow motion, she screamed as, with arms outstretched, she turned in the air, over and over. Crashing down in a shower of spray she saw the water turned red beneath them. Then the noise from the crowd was muffled as Kelly's weight drove the breath from her body as he pushed her into the silt of the lakebed.

James felt his love turn, then she gave a muffed cry of anguish as if in a nightmare. As her battered and bruised face nestled close to his, he cradled her tenderly and vowed to protect her against all harm in the wilderness under the stars.

A soft wind blew ruffling and distorted the image.

The water felt warm and held her buoyant, and the smell, the powerful odour was of her one and only love. Katrina whimpered twice now that the nightmare had gone, and the pain that was with her had disappeared. Safe now that her inner senses had recognised her protector was with her, she lapsed from her semi-conscious state into the darkness of complete oblivion. Holding her lightly with both hands, and close to him, he breathed across her face to reassure her that he was with her. Unable to refuel the fire, he watched mesmerised as the flames slowly abated until only the bright embers glowed in the blackness. Fickle moon had again succumbed to the cloud cover, although his eyes had acquired a certain amount of night vision. By now, all his senses were fully alert to any unusual sound or intrusion.

The ambulance siren sounded its wailing cry at least two miles away as it negotiated the narrow lanes, and he plotted its winding course into the village where Alan would be urgently waiting to guide it to her. That sound had completely overwhelmed him with emotion. Now the tension, like an over-stretched banjo string was broken. The knowledge that within a few minutes his love would be whisked away from him was too much for his sensitive nature to bear. Sobbing, he gently rocked the limp figure as tears rolled down his face uncontrollably, cutting channels through the congealed blood on her.

Then they came—not two pairs of lights but six. Even from his position on the ground the whole sky seemed to glow and reflect the canopy of brightness moving slowly towards them. James wanted to lift her bodily and run to shorten the distance between them, but he paused, then lay back quietly. He had seen her tumble from the horse but not clearly; his love could have bones broken. Then he noticed the absent hard hat, and felt paralysed and numb with shock. The paramedics' questions were direct, and he tried to give them answers that would help. The most surprising thing to him was that though only a short time had elapsed since his confrontation with the unknown rider, for him it was a lifetime.

Alan moved closer to the crouching figure. There was a question that needed an answer. "James…" He touched his arm to draw his attention. Already a collar had been attached to Katrina's neck, and now they were checking professionally for any broken limbs. The watcher never answered. He was trying to listen for any words spoken by the medics, to ascertain in his own mind how physically injured the figure on the stretcher might be.

Moving closer, again he spoke almost in a whisper: "James, when I drove to get help did you hear the sound of a shotgun?"

James was not remotely interested in who fired the shots. All his thoughts were directed towards the doors of the ambulance now closing. Then a strange thought came, and for the first time that evening he felt very humble and vulnerable. For all his great strength, he had been no match for the jealous workings of a mind.

All the damage inflicted on Katrina was this unknown assailant's doing, and if his feelings were correct, then he had paid the ultimate price. He clenched his fist, and tensed his muscles, sending the blood coursing through his veins—no one would whip a dog like that—so that when he turned, the power in his tone implied that he already knew the answer. "Above the tree line, towards your sheep-shearing barn."

"Two blasts."

"Bristol, near the M32," someone called, as her transport lumbered off, leaving him with a number of strangers, prying for information as to what had happened.

"James, you go now, we will take care of this end. If you get a chance to speak to Katrina tell her that Kelly is okay."

"Thanks, Alan."

"Don't thank me, you're the one who drove him off. George and Catherine will be for ever in your debt, now clear off."

Turning away he shouted across to a colleague, "Harry, have you raised Katrina's parents on that mobile phone yet?"

The answer was in the negative, but the owner swore that he would try every few minutes, and that was accepted by the others. When the convoy of four-wheel-drive vehicles moved towards the track leading to the barn, headlamps blazing, the lonely giant gathered pace into a frantic run, going the other way towards his car, still parked under the trees. Within minutes the Ford

Escort was powering through the lanes, and, all the time he was driving, his thoughts dwelled on the brief sight of his love framed in the lighted door of the ambulance. Should he have gone with her? Every instinct had told him to rush over and climb in the vehicle, but her parents could be waiting at the entrance to the valley, and his appearance was not inspiring, to say the least. The nearer his destination, the more nervous and worried he became, as his stomach knotted and turned over and over.

Finding a place in the car park was easy at that time of night. Without even locking the car, he ran towards the casualty department. Many heads turned in the crowded waiting room as he burst in like a huge tornado, and a shocked silence descended on the area. Eyes that had been examining cuts or bruises, or reading the scattered magazines a second ago, were now firmly focused on the new arrival—bare torso with muscles bulging, accentuated by the red, angry-looking weals across his body, smoke-blackened face sporting a dark purple and blue scuff mark from his ear to his mouth; huge pupils not yet dilated, set in large shining blue eyes that stared back unflinching. Everyone in the room came to their own conclusion as to what he was. Most settled for lager lout, or even clockwork-orange renegade. The receptionist looked at his dirt-stained hands, the damaged face with the sweat running down from his hair, and pulled back as she tried to make sense of what he was saying. "Can I help you?"

From her office the duty casualty sister had seen the agitation on his face, and like many others whom she had met dishevelled and dirty, her experience over the years had taught her that first impressions were usually well wide of the mark.

"Katrina, I must see her now, where is she?"

"Who are you inquiring for?" She was looking at the new intakes. "Miss Chambers?"

"That's right," he almost shouted, "Katrina how is she? I want to see her."

"Are you family?"

He half-turned away in frustration and began to drum his large fingers on the wooden reception counter top.

"If you go into the waiting room I will try and find some information for you as soon as possible."

Others were already phoning asking for news on the girl, and she wondered how big a part the large, now seated figure had to play in the drama. When the paramedics had brought her into casualty it had looked like a serious motor vehicle accident. Then they told their tale of how they had found her in the wilderness in the arms of a naked giant who had growled at them. But the whip lashes were everywhere, so some of their story was true at least.

The phone rang on the desk. "Casualty, can I help?"

The reply was the standard "satisfactory"—not that there was any news to give; that was the tenth call in as many minutes. Who *is* Katrina Chambers?

Behind the scenes the doctor was looking at the results of the X-rays intently. No bones had been broken, and as far as they could tell there were no internal injuries. Most of her wounds were superficial and not life-threatening, although the one across her forehead would need stitching, as would the two down the side of her face. They had wiped the clotted blood from her eyes, but her hair was still matted dark red against the snowy-white pillow. Every now and again her eyes flickered open, but no light pierced her darkness, so there was no sight in them.

James sat head down, hands on each side of his face, completely oblivious to the noise or the other dramas being played out around him. All of his thoughts were for his love's recovery.

Ten o'clock came and he was still sat rigid in the chair staring into space. Briefly he came out of his shell to ask if there was any news, then he reverted to the same position. Eleven came and went, and so had the family. Even Richard who had driven down from London in record time had not seen him in the corner of the waiting room. They were allowed in the intensive care unit for only a brief moment as the doctors were still somewhat baffled by her comatose stupor. Now she lay blissfully unaware of being monitored by the latest technical equipment. Twelve, the midnight hour—he had been waiting almost three hours without any real news at all. Now the area was fairly quiet, with only one or two waiting for their partners to return from the treatment room after having their ailments dressed.

He stood up and walked towards the small office. "Tell Katrina that I will be waiting outside. My name is James, I will be in the car park. When she is ready I will take her home."

The sister bit her lip. "It is no good you waiting, the young lady will be with us all night."

He moved closer towards her and she felt the power and anger radiating from his body. "I will sleep in the car park, and take her home with me in the morning then."

The sister watched as he dialled a number, then shook her head as she walked away. There was a spare bed at one time that could have been offered, but now it had been taken.

"Dad, it's me." He tried to take any emotion from his voice. "I'm at the local hospital, I won't be home tonight, Katrina's had an accident."

"James, are you both all right?"

"There is nothing wrong with me. That's why I am waiting; they won't let me see her yet."

Betty, who was listening, shook her head, then whispered to John, "You had better drive over and find out what's going on—get him home if you can."

Twelve minutes later he entered the door, then froze as he saw the state of his son who had been unaware of his entry.

Within two more minutes, he had obtained the information that the girl was in the intensive care unit, and no visitors were allowed except immediate family. "James, the sister said that if you go home now, and come back in the morning, there is a good chance that you will be allowed to visit Katrina for a few minutes, what do you say?"

"Why are you here? Go away and leave me alone."

The dark scowling figure waved his arms, emphasising his point.

One of the passing hospital porters paused, as he saw the drama, taking place: "All okay, Sister?"

"Yes, it's all right, carry on."

How many times in the past had she witnessed high emotions as loved ones waited in frustration, as they realised that they could do nothing to help.

"Young man, come with me, I can't give you permission to enter, but if you are unobtrusive, you can see her briefly from the doorway.

The half-darkened room bristled with monitors sending out coloured signals. From his vantage point, the beds were just a misty haze, with beads of light flickering across the wires that connected to them. Katrina was there—he could feel her presence—but, which one encradled her, there was no way of knowing. Then he moved away, and gave a heavy sigh. There was no more that he could do—he had come, he had seen, now he must go. It was as simple as that—only one more thing he could do, he could pray for a speedy recovery.

"Thank you, thank you."

Out went a large grubby hand that was declined by his benefactor, who gave a wry smile as she looked at her own pristine scrubbed fingers. They almost marched along the short corridor together until James nodded to his father to join him, just as his companion peeled off and entered her own domain.

"Right then, what do we have now? Broken finger,

broken toe, broken heart?" Taking the admittance cards from the reception box she looked to the ceiling. "What a job!" she muttered as, shaking her head, she walked briskly into the room where the last few patients were waiting.

Betty watched her son walk across the lawn from his car, climb the steps, and move out of her way as he entered the lighted lobby. Not saying a word, he entered the bathroom and turned on the shower. Close behind came John who didn't speak either, but she could tell by his grim face that something awful had happened. Where was his shirt, the one he only wore on special occasions, and what were those dark stains across his body? Then she felt queasy—not blood, there was too much of it.

"John!" She rushed into the kitchen. "What has happened?"

"I honestly don't know. Katrina is in the intensive care unit and has been there for a number of hours, so it must have been early in the evening."

"Only—" he pointed towards the bathroom "—can tell us what brought her into this state, and at the moment he is too shocked to say anything. "There was a brief instant at the hospital when I almost believed that he was going to strike me."

James set the water temperature almost unbearably hot, and let the jets burn into his skin. When he emerged fifteen minutes later he was glowing. Gone were the stains from the night's episode, washed away in a flood of steam. Slowly they had disappeared in a miniature whirlpool down the plug hole, and with them his energy had seemed to evaporate. Now all he wanted to do was crawl into bed and think of her. The bedside clock showed one-twenty-four a.m., and his tangled thoughts tried to slot into place what day it was. There was no need to set the alarm for the morning, as he knew that at seven-thirty his father would make enough noise in the kitchen to wake him. Sometimes he was lucky, most times not—the dog jumped on the bed and snuggled down contentedly as the hand patted the cover. James wanted company tonight, and his four-legged friend was more than happy to oblige. Within minutes both fell into a fitful sleep.

John only dozed. He was waiting, and when the dog barked and snarled even before the bell rang, he knew that they had come. Now he would know the truth of whatever events had taken place last evening. That was why he had not pressurised his boy; he could sit back as an observer, and just listen while other people asked the questions. James went through the motions of how he had disarmed the attacker, and how he had believed that his assailant's leg was broken, and how Alan from the stables had called for the ambulance.

Only a few questions: "Yes, we had arranged to meet in the valley. No, I had never seen the rider before."

They thanked him for his co-operation and went off with the signed statement, adding the parting comment there was a possibility that they would call again. James watched the police car pull away, shrugged his shoulders, walked into his bedroom, disrobed, and rolled back into bed. John made a cup of tea for his wife, coffee for himself, strolled purposely into bedroom, sat on the bed and related their son's heroic deeds.

George was up early. He had already phoned the hospital: yes, there was an improvement. On the matter of a private ward, again the answer was positive. Now he and Richard were looking over Kelly; the vet had finished his examination and passed the horse AI. They were both pleased first and foremost for Katrina, then for the added bonus that there was no damage to the stallion. Catherine and Josie were in the kitchen and the latter was trying discreetly to raise the subject of her forthcoming wedding. Both his mother and father had said that they would not go, not now that Katrina was in hospital. Then the two men returned looking a lot happier than when they had gone out.

Josie grabbed her future husband: "The wedding, what about the wedding?"

Richard pulled her to him. "There's no need to worry; we'll all fly out together next week as planned."

"Are you sure?"

"Have I been wrong yet?"

"You are a cocky..." She wanted to say bastard, but settled for so-and-so, as Catherine was near by.

Katrina felt the slight pain as the light grew stronger, then one eye came into focus on the unfamiliar ceiling above her head. Then a face that seemed a long distance away came closer until it completely blotted out anything else. Why was it so dark on her right side? Then she started to shake as the nightmare returned—her right eye had been damaged; she was without sight in that eye, that was the reason she could not see.

Mind-numbing fear gripped her whole body. "I'm blind, I'm blind!" she screamed. "Let me out, I must go home."

"Hush, you've had stitches, it's just the covering has slipped slightly." Deft hands adjusted the offending wad quickly. "There, is that better?"

Katrina did not answer; her thoughts were already racing ahead. There were many questions to ask, and things to do. James, why was he not with her last evening? Or was he? Kelly, Badminton—must go, so much to do. She tried to lever herself up on the bed, but found her strength wanting, so she lay back trying to gather together all the pieces of the jigsaw. Everything seemed to be moving fast from her awaking—nurses, doctors, pain, all jumbled together. There had been the questions from the police, the utter terror of the night before. The private ward, compliments of her father, was light and airy, with flowers strategically placed around for her comfort. Midday saw her pluck up courage to look at her reflection in a mirror. The face staring back was not hers; it was misshapen, ugly. Dark purple in colour, with the right side of her face twisted out of proportion, she could see, although the large pad covered most of the damage, that the swelling had closed most of her eye. Katrina started to perspire: no, he could never love someone looking like this, only pity her, and that was not for her.

By two o'clock in the afternoon she could stand the built-up tension no longer. George her father took the connection, then listened intently to his daughter's words; they were short and to the point. "Father, organise Kelly for Badminton, then get me out of here, I train tomorrow."

Not waiting for a reply, she put down the receiver, then took it off the hook. Even if anyone wanted to call, she had effectively stopped them. Grim-faced she went back into the nightmare: if only they could clear the fence at the lake everything would be all right, and there was only one way to find out and that was to face the bogey head on. Two hours later Katrina was locking the door of her bedroom in the Wiltshire village, but not before giving precise instructions that she would speak to no one.

On Tuesday he had been denied entrance to the ward in the morning, and the day had been long and painful for him; the only information he could glean was "satisfactory". Now he was ready at six-thirty in the evening to force a visit if necessary.

James burnished his shoes for the third time, looked at his watch for the tenth time in as many minutes, walked into the bathroom and adjusted his tie, then returned to the same to clean his teeth. There was no training session tomorrow as the first team was playing in the Midlands, so his plan was to visit Katrina, then go into their small print shop and help his father.

Again he looked at the watch. Only his mother had stopped him rushing out to the hospital early: "They are having their tea on the wards, and they will not let you in until they're finished, so sit down and do the same." Then later, "Go on, you will drive me mad, if you don't stop walking around, don't forget the flowers."

Betty brushed a loose hair from the suit's coat; he did look handsome, and his eyes that were dull and lifeless when he emerged in the morning, were now beginning to sparkle in anticipation of his meeting.

The receptionist watched as the figure walk towards her nervously, clutching a large handful of flowers, a visitor, but much too early to be let loose on the wards. Then he smiled and the two dark blue lagoons seemed to swallow her whole, so that any reservations about not letting him through vanished in an instant.

"Katrina Chambers."

Before he could utter another word, they were filled in for him. Not another one, twelve phone calls, two police officers in person, now this gorgeous young man, and the young woman was not even in the hospital. "I'm sorry but Miss Chambers is not with us."

"Another hospital, which one?" he questioned as an anxious frown settled on his pleading face, "Katrina is all right?"

The words were soft and gentle with a depth and tone that made the listener wince. Then she knew that this was the half-naked blood-smeared giant whom the paramedics had spoken of almost in awe. What was his name? Come on, come on, the ward sister told you this morning, quick, quick!

"No, James, Katrina has gone home." His name rolled off her tongue powerfully, while the last four words drifted off in a down-beat, fading away fashion, as if to say, I am here. The long-stemmed roses were held close to his face, as if he was savouring their fragrance, covered the wide grin. Even if the girl was flirting with him, his euphoric thoughts were far away in a small village, where his one and only love would be resting from her ordeal. Now all he wanted to do was run outside and punch the air with delight. Half-turning away from the desk, he paused, took a single flower from the bunch, kissed it once, gave a big wink, and passed it across to the slender waiting hand. Happiness should be shared, his mother had always drummed into him, and he hoped superstitiously that this small gesture now would help him when he talked to his love.

Eagerly wanting to hear her sweet voice again, he found it almost impossible to keep within the thirty-mile speed limit as he drove the short distance to his home. Eagerly anticipating her reaction to his call, the steps outside the entrance to the bungalow were taken in two strides. From the bunch rattling in his hand, the appropriate key, grasped tightly between finger and thumb, already pointing forward, slipped easily into the lock; a twist of his wrist and he was inside the door.

Brushing his mother's question aside, he grabbed the phone and dialled her home. "Answer, Katrina, answer, my love," he said out loud for the burr-burr seemed to go on for ever as he waited impatiently for his connection.

Click! All the blood drained from his tanned face, and he looked at the instrument in a daze as the monitored answering machine informed him that no one was available to take the call. Shaken to the core, all his hopes in ashes, it took a few moments to think of what to say while the moving, cold, unfeeling blank tape waited unconcerned for his words at the other end of the line.

"James, it's James, hope you…"

He was lost, should he say, "are recovered" or "get well"? The words stuck in his throat; all he wanted to do was hold her in his arms and let the strength from him heal her.

"I will call later this evening, or if you can give me a bell…? Love James."

There was no need to leave the word love on the tape, it could cause problems, but what the hell, her parents should know his feelings. Even if he had made a mistake unconsciously, there was no way that the tape could be erased from his end now. The hours passed quickly, almost too quick, and as there had been no reply to his call he could only contemplate that his love was not there.

Wednesday morning, Richard drove the car along the roads and tracks, so that Katrina could inspect and evaluate the degree of difficulty facing her on Saturday. Although he had offered her his hand on a number of occasions, it had been declined almost with disdain. It was almost as if she was trying to self-destruct as she walked the course.

Katrina clenched her teeth as the loose earth moved away from under the wood fence, forcing her hand to hang on for a few seconds' support while she regained her balance. Pain was a blessing: it focused her mind completely on the task ahead. Each main obstacle was inspected thoroughly, and the alternative safer route analysed on the long cross-country course. Richard kept close beside her, keeping away colleagues or friends who might intrude unintentionally on her vowed solitude. Just a few words were enough, and only from a distance did they call a greeting. There were no secrets between the two of them, and he had told her in no uncertain terms that to ride was not only foolish but downright suicidal. Frostily, she had rejected his advice, with the added words that if she wanted to kill herself it was her problem, not his.

Now he was reluctantly driving her towards more agony, as Kelly was safely installed at the Badminton stables, and it was her intention to be with him as soon as possible.

"Kiddo, are you going to talk to James today?" Something was definitely wrong, there had been no mention of her young man even to him.

"No." The word was sharp, frosty and final.

"Katrina," he almost shouted, "when will you call him, this evening?"

"No, I will not." She stamped her foot to empathise the point.

Richard was shocked. How could his sister become so ice cold and bitter towards the one person that he knew she dearly loved.

"Why the hell are you here, Kiddo? You should be thanking him for saving your miserable life, I know that, Mother, Father, everyone in the village—we all can't be wrong, can we?"

Pausing only for a second to take a deep breath, and to make sure that the car was still on the right track he pushed on. "Rodrick's dead, you're only battered, with everything to live for, so tell me why? So I can try to understand."

"Look at me," she screamed. "Look at my face, how could he love someone so ugly?"

That was the problem—he had guessed rightly, but wanted his sister to let go her bottled-up emotions. Now it was a case of finding a solution that would benefit all concerned.

"Kiddo, you are still lovely, and you know that I would not lie. Within two weeks it will be just like a bad dream, then your beauty will bewitch everyone as it always has." Soft came the words like honey to soothe her troubled, scarred mind.

Katrina sat stiff in the seat; no emotion showed on her face, but her hands were twisting the seat belts as her inner demons played havoc with her thoughts. Richard slowed to a crawl: he could go on giving her compliments, but there was an alternative: blackmail—although he knew even that was a gamble.

"Okay, you cannot cope with speaking on the phone. I'm here to keep people away from you, that's fine. We will drive across to the marshall's tent and scrub out your name. There is no way that you could even think of riding with the thousands milling around the course in the next few days, not with your attitude. It's too dangerous, for them, and yourself."

Bull's eye, first shot! The colour started from her neck, then slowly intensified as it spread upwards, so that all of her face came into a bright crimson bloom. Katrina felt the heat generated by the pointed dart that had wounded her pride, but, unknown to her brother, the warmth had stirred deep feelings within her. Eyes closed so that the vision would be enhanced, she felt the breath from his mouth burn like fire as he sought her moist lips, then as brief as it came so it faded.

But in those moments she had been reborn. Gone was the resolve to keep her love away until they returned from Barbados; there was one thing that she could do that would show everyone how much she would sacrifice for him. Even Richard, who was her champion, would never agree to her plan, which had been formulated in a blinding flash of inspiration only a few seconds ago.

"Richard, you call James this evening." Steel-like was the tone of her voice. "Tell him to stay away from the event, I need all my concentration to be fully focused. I will phone him on Friday late."

The fake iron deception almost crumbled as the last short sentence came to her lips, but a jolt from the car made her wince, only helping her slip out the words without giving away any of the feelings she felt. "Oh, you can say that I give him all my love."

Richard nodded in agreement. At least there would be some contact; he knew how the young man felt, even if his cold-hearted sister didn't. Katrina had already sent instructions that Kelly was to be saddled and ready for her. As they drove into the car park close to the stables, Mary Joe, as was her nature, wanted to run out and console her friend striding purposely towards her, but faded discreetly into the shadows as she drew near. Following, grim-faced, walked her brother.

Katrina checked her stallion thoroughly, and the hidden watcher witnessed just a faint smile light up her face briefly as she walked him around to warm up. Then she mounted and rode off across the wide swathes of green towards the trees, leaving Richard, standing hands-in-pocket, watching their progress intently. James was not happy at all. He was sat sipping a hot cup of coffee in his father's workshop, and contemplating the total chaos that was taxing his thoughts to the utmost.

Within a few days, if you counted six-fifteen in the afternoon as almost a completed day, his nice, safe, easy world had been turned completely upside down. From being one of the boys—have a few beers, go to the local football match, go out when he wanted, come home ditto, have a laugh at other people's expense, of course—life was suddenly very serious. Now his mother was manning the telephone; on pain of death dare she go out. His father for the first two hours in the morning had hardly said a word, then had disappeared on the pretence of visiting customers, and had not returned. He was totally in love, completely in the dark, and so frustrated that it hurt.

Should he drive to the village, find her house and demand information, why had he not done this already? Three times in the day he had climbed into the Ford Escort with this explicit intention, and then found some excuse why he should not. Alan who owned Home Farm? He should know where Katrina had gone, the hospital had implicitly said home; if that was the case surely she would have made contact by now? James put down the unfinished drink, and walked into the office. Thumbing through the directory, he breathed a sigh of relief as he found the farm listed. Resting one hand on the desk for support, James steeled himself for the bad news that he had convinced himself would soon manifest itself, then he dialled the number.

When the connection was made there was no need to ask how his love was faring, it came crystal-clear over the line, without him even asking. "Tony, is that you?—I mean James. Where have you been today? Katrina is in one hell of a mess where he whipped her—a black eye, and her face is swollen something awful on one side, must have hit the ground with a mighty thump. Her brother Richard is with her, probably to keep the press away. You heard about Rodrick, killed the horse as well, bastard. Busy are you? Probably see you tomorrow, if you can get away from work, or definitely on Friday as Katrina competes in the dressage on the second day. Anyway, why am I rambling on? Katrina would have given you all the news, thanks for what you did, everyone wants to meet you, see you soon."

James looked in astonishment at the dead receiver—he had not said a word but had been given the information without even asking. The only thing that puzzled him greatly was why had Katrina not phoned. Alan had said that they had been drawn to ride in the dressage on Friday: at least that would give her more time to recover. That was great news really: he could finish training tomorrow morning and drive straight to Badminton and see her. As her involvement in the competition did not start until the Friday, at least they could have an hour or two walking the course together. After locking the print shop, he drove home in a happier frame of mind than he'd had all day; his love was okay and he was going to see her tomorrow.

Richard was tired. All the family were exhausted; they had had very little sleep for the last two nights worrying over Katrina's injuries and now they and even Richard was ready for bed. There was one important call that must be made before he could retire, although how the pill could be sweetened by him calling and not his sister completely baffled him.

Brief *News at Ten* on Channel Five had just started on the television when the sound that he had been waiting for made James leap from the chair and run into the hall. Betty, who had watched the strange non-events throughout the day, had spent most of the evening in the kitchen trying to fathom out how a well-brought-up young lady whom her son had saved from a severe beating, or worse, could be so callous as not to speak to him. Another hospital? Brain damage was her immediate thought but this was discounted as soon as the message came back that the girl had been riding all day.

James pulled up sharply. His mother was holding the receiver and talking to someone. Betty motioned for him to take over. "It's Katrina's brother."

James listened intently as Richard gave him a first-rate briefing, listing all the salient points from the time he had received the phone call in London. He recounted the family's visit to the hospital, the extent of Katrina's injuries, and her obsession to compete at Badminton. The one thing he didn't mention was why his sister, who was prowling around him with a heavy frown on her face, was not giving this information.

"Richard—" Of her training throughout the day he knew already from Alan, so breaking in on the speaker to ask the relevant question that had tested him so sorely was more than justified. "Why have you called and not Katrina?"

The girl saw her brother's eyelids narrow, and she moved closer as he paused. Talking to people of all ranks in the army was a routine task for him, so that when his sister had demanded that it was almost his duty to help her he had acquiesced. The question now asked had been at the forefront of his mind when figuring out what he would say to James. Now he would speak, knowing his sister was listening, but making sure that James would believe what he was going to say.

"What I am going to tell you is strictly between you and me—not even my parents know. If anyone suspects, Katrina will be barred from competing. Are you listening?"

Richard said the last sentence more for the attention of the white-faced statue watching him than James.

"I believe that the fall from the horse has slightly disoriented her mind. Now she hates everyone including me. The message from her is that you must not try and communicate, and under no circumstances attend the competition."

Richard paused for a second, then, as there was no reply, carried on.

"The best thing to do, James, is to forget all about her for now, and maybe call in a few weeks' time when Katrina returns from the wedding. Don't take it personally, Kiddo is not speaking to anyone, and I do mean no one—we have had one bitch of a day. Thanks for taking care of our Kid the other evening, from all of us. See you around, any message you want passing on?" Richard watched as his silent agitated sister mouthed the words, "Tell James I love him."

Then he shook his head slowly, closed his eyes so that her antics would not impinge on his thoughts as the faltering words came down the line. "Tell Katrina that I lo—v—e her, and hope her and Kelly do well."

Click, the connection was broken. Richard opened his eyes wide, shrugged his shoulders, then looked at his sister as if to say, "I never severed the line, you can't blame me."

Katrina was shaking with anger, and her finger was pointing at her brother like a dagger. "Why did you not say that I loved him, or that he could expect a phone call on Friday? It was most important."

Richard grinned. "There you are." He gestured towards the dead instrument: "You do it! By the way, lover boy wishes you well at Badminton, and gives you all his love. I don't know why; he must be mad, what do you think?"

Katrina stopped herself rising to his misguided banter, and suddenly for no apparent reason she felt totally weary. Her antagonist saw the slump in her shoulders, and knew that the adrenaline that had fuelled her all day was almost exhausted. Quickly he slipped his hand around her waist and, supporting her weight, propelled her up the stairs. Catherine heard them coming and guided her daughter into the bathroom where some tepid warm water would help soothe her ills. The mirror on the cabinet Katrina totally ignored, preferring not to inspect for any improvement or deterioration. All she was interested in was washing thoroughly, drying carefully, and then crawling into bed gratefully.

Thirty minutes later with no dreams or nightmares to torment her, and her breathing soft and regular Katrina slipped into a deep sleep. James glanced at his watch—just a couple of minutes into Thursday morning went through his thoughts. Then looking at the soft clouds scudding across the moon, he took a deep breath, and settled down to the start of a steady ten-mile circular run. Space and freedom to think—that was the answer. And, as his legs moved into a rhythm, covering the ground effortlessly, so his thoughts dwelt on the information that he had received. Two miles out, he had the answer, two more and he was not so sure, six, the problem was still with him, and his pounding feet still beat the tattoo, she loves me, she loves me not, hammering into his scarred emotions. Now he was holding on to the gatepost at the end of his self-imposed punishment, legs like jelly, wishing that his tremendous love for her would overcome any hidden barriers between them. There was one thing that he had noticed over and over again. Ever since he had met the girl his life seemed to be run by his watch; now it was two o'clock in the morning, his plan was to drive to Badminton before eight, and he had not even gone to bed yet.

Half an hour later after a silent shower and a brisk rub-down with a rough towel in the half-darkness, he at last pulled the duvet over his naked body and worried. "Blast!" He was late; no sleep the night before, hardly any in the last few hours. He knew it would catch up with him but why this morning when he needed the time most? All he wanted to do was to find the best vantage point, so that he could watch his love compete on Friday without her knowing that he was there. James hurriedly dressed in the full regalia of his keeper's outfit; at least that would save time at the training ground later. He folded his shirt, trousers and tie into a sports bag, then moved towards the front door.

"James, James, don't you want any breakfast?" Betty called after the fleeing figure.

There was no answer, and she looked across at her husband who shrugged his shoulders. "I don't know what he's up to. At least he is going to football. Maybe he will come in to work later."

The rider forced herself to stay in bed, even though the exciting thought that half her competitors were waiting for the start of the dressage tried to lure her from it. For months she had been rising at dawn. Now her willing helper would be mucking out the stable and overseeing Kelley's needs, so there was no need to rush anywhere. There were a few who would score highly in this discipline today; they would be riding later, and Katrina knew that then was the time to watch her main rivals. The oblong, blue-black tinted face staring back at her from the bathroom mirror was not hers, but today her hair hung down, not platted into the usual pony-tail, so that by brushing it forward the sides of her face were covered. Although the new improvised style did not improve her looks, in her opinion at least most of the damage was hidden from view. Katrina slipped the silk night-dress over her shoulders gingerly and let it slide slowly down her body to lie in a crumpled heap around her feet. Red weals crossed her smooth tanned skin. Although the pain had been excruciating, her thick woollen sweater had partially protected her from the leather thong's cutting edge. Only the slashes down the face and the one on her forehead had drawn blood.

"Katrina." It was her mother calling, and before another word was uttered, the face in the mirror smiled and whispered sweetly, "Are you coming down to breakfast?" in perfect harmony with the caller.

"Five minutes, Mother." Her voice was strong and direct, with just a hint of "I will come when I'm ready". There was no doubt that she felt stronger and more in control of her emotions this morning, so there would be no more hiding from her friends, press, or fellow competitors. The only person that she could not face was the one who had fought for her and won. Her love for him was much too deep and overwhelming to chance that he would reject her now. Soon the time would come that would prove that she placed him above all her material wealth, and only then would she feel that she had in part repaid what he had done for her. Dressing unhurriedly, so that her thoughts could dwell on other matters than her own plight, she remembered that her brother was bringing Josie for her first visit to Badminton this morning. One last peek at her smiling reflection, and she vacated the bathroom and clattered hurriedly down the stairs.

Richard was just rising from the breakfast table as his sister appeared. "Tea, coffee, toast with marmalade, cereal? You look a million dollars this morning, doesn't she, Mother?"

"There's a definite improvement from yesterday, but are you sure that you're well enough to ride tomorrow?"

"Mother, I'm fine. Come on then, Richard, pour the tea."

The one thing that she dreaded most was a long inquisition about how she was feeling. Throughout the short time they were together at the table, Katrina tried and succeeded in steering the conversation away from herself, and onto the more interesting subject of the forthcoming marriage. Her brother had driven quickly down from London with his bride-to-be as soon as the message that she was in hospital was received, and they were still here. Now this morning she felt guilty that it was she that was taking up too much of her brother's time and not Josie.

"Richard?"

He looked across the breakfast table with that infuriating half-smile, and she knew instantly that her thoughts had been silently stolen away, and that he knew already the words that she would have spoken.

"Nothing."

One eyebrow rose a fraction, then the other, but she stared into his eyes, not giving ground or information. If he knew already, what was the point? Ten minutes later Katrina was waiting impatiently in the doorway for the two of them to join her.

"You carry on, Kiddo, we will drive over later." Richard grinned wickedly.

Her shoulders slumped—game set and match. He had finalised in seconds the thoughts that had been troubling her for hours.

"Are you sure that it is wise, to let Katrina ride alone today?"

"Mother, she's okay. I can assure you that most of the day will be spent watching her rivals, not from the back of Kelly, but on her own two feet. By the way, around lunch time we're driving back to London. There are a few things we need to tie up before tonight. Then we'll return in the morning to watch Katrina. If there was the slightest chance that Katrina needed any more chaperoning we would not go."

"I wish your father was here. At least you could reassure him first-hand, rather than me trying on the telephone later."

Richard nodded briefly in reply. His thoughts were already on another subject as through the window he watched the green MG power up the hill.

"Come on, Josie, let's go hunting."

Catherine looked at her son in astonishment, so did Josie. Even with her limited knowledge of riding there was no doubt in her mind that when the first hedge loomed in front of her, the only way past would be through a gate.

They were both wrong. One hour four minutes and twenty seconds later, Richard spotted his quarry. Katrina was engrossed in watching the dressage, so they had spoken only a few words to her before moving out from the gathered spectators into the open. One sweep with his powerful binoculars over the open parkland had brought an instant reward. There was no mistake. Barbour waterproof jackets, in all shades of green or brown, some old, others worn for the first time this morning; tweeds of all colours, woollen jumpers of different hues, mixed and blended neatly around the arena, giving an impression of perfect harmony. Approximately one hundred and forty metres away like the dark hole in an almost completed jigsaw with one piece missing to mar the scene, lay the still figure of a man. Yellow and black goalkeeper's shirt, with the number one emblazoned down the back, jet-black tracksuit bottoms tucked into black and white ringed socks—this had to be him. Richard walked with Josie hand-in-hand towards the prone statue. As they drew nearer it was obvious that his attention was not on the event, but on the crowd watching.

James adjusted the focus of his magnifying glasses slightly as Katrina moved to another position.

Sitting up quickly, he acknowledged the nod from the lead walker as they both passed within a yard of where he was watching.

Richard saw the glint of gold from the unusual torque

necklace around James' neck, and almost faltered in his stride. Then he knew for sure how deeply his sister must love this young man deeply, and he was glad.

"Josie, there's no need for us to return tomorrow. We'll come down early Saturday morning, that will give you more than enough time to raid the supermarket stores."

"But...Katrina. You promised to watch her ride in the dressage tomorrow morning."

"There is no need. Someone much more important than us will be close by supporting her, not to mention Mother and Father and all the villagers around. Look." Passing the binoculars, he pointed at the now standing figure.

"Richard, you devil. That's the reason you said we were going hunting, you knew that he'd be here. How do you do it?"

He laughed. "Easy, that's exactly how I would have reacted."

"Do you think that Katrina knows he's watching?"

"No, and we'll not be around to tell her. Come on, we can leave now, nothing can stop the two of them coming together very soon."

"How can you be so sure?"

The knuckles on his hands turned white as he gripped the iron rail tightly, while his thoughts briefly spanned the past. The unexpected phone message had given him instructions to call on a law firm, and he had opened the package given to him in front of the solicitor with intrigue.

There lay the gold Roman torque, the one that he had found in the valley when he was sixteen, and given to his first and always remembered love. The value was in thousands of pounds now, but at the time it was their secret, just the two of them bonded together by its brightness and beauty. Then the family had vanished, almost overnight, and it was much later that the truth came out that his father had bought the farm, and that they had gone across the world to New Zealand.

Richard knew that he needed to ask questions of the solicitor, but his mind was completely numb. Despite having searched for her in the past, it had been to no avail. Now it was over—meningitis had taken her.

Within minutes of leaving the solicitor's office he had on impulse begun to drive down to Wiltshire, to pass on what was dear to him. That had been at least four, perhaps even five years ago. Now his sister had parted with the love token, and he was not only pleased, but proud of her.

"I just know. Don't ask me why, something, a feeling, call it what you like. One thing's for sure, they are very, very close."

Katrina was so engrossed in the competition as she followed one of the English riders went through her routine that her brother's faint words fell on deaf ears as they passed her by. Later it came as a shock when her mother explained that they had returned home, and were not coming back until Saturday morning. Four or five times in the evening her hand had hovered over the phone, but she had failed to find the courage to ring James' number. Why the torture? You know he will not want you, just forget him. Her mind was a mass of little thoughts magnified into big doubts, all rolling around in a ball throwing off ice-cold splinters to wound her, making her face almost a set mask.

Usually the night before a competition there would be plenty of laughter while the three of them discussed the merits of the other riders, and the state of the ground that she would compete on. Although they had worked as a team in order to get everything ready for the biggest test of her life the next morning, Katrina seemed only to be going through the motions, without any spark in what she did.

Again her hand hovered, then withdrew.

"Good night," Katrina called loudly, and quickly mounted the stairs in case anyone asked why so early.

Pulling back her hair, she looked at the reflection of her face in the mirror. Red parallel lines ran from her forehead down her face almost to her throat. They were crossed neatly with plastic stitches holding her wounds together. Tomorrow was her big day, and all she could see was a railtrack running down her face, making her ugly.

Gingerly, she slipped into bed, and lay back facing the ceiling with her head high on the pillow, projecting her thoughts well into the next morning. He would be watching, she was sure of it now. That was why her brother had gone back to London; James had been in the park today. She smiled; bastard Richard, why had he not told her? Of course he had known that she would guess, as she always did. Then she laughed and cried at the same time, and as the pent-up bitterness washed from her eyes. Whatever happened on the day, it would work out.

11

The morning dawned a chilly cold one, and a grey mist completely shrouded the village. Katrina shivered as she looked from her half-opened bedroom window at the over-large spider's web, etched out in gossamer white by the early morning dew, its dark keeper, like the trap, clearly visible, even for the most unwary.

From the door came a light tap, then a pause, as if the person did not want to intrude on the occupant. Smiling, she scuttled across the room, still shivering but now more in anticipation of the day's event than the cold.

"Mother you can come in." Her tone was pleasant and welcoming, which almost surprised her, as the evening before she had definitely felt jumpy.

Catherine felt the warmth even in those few words as she entered the room. There was a lot that she wanted to say, but she knew that her daughter was headstrong when it came to riding. Pulling out now would not have even entered her head. Funny that the fellow from

Bristol had not been mentioned. She frowned—odd that Richard was not with them today either.

Katrina watched her mother who was standing still and staring, with a preoccupied look on her face.

"Mother, are you all right?"

"Yes dear." Catherine shook her head as if to clear her thoughts. "Your father has suggested that we all go together, of course if you prefer to go on your own, we resp—"

Katrina broke in: "Fine, tell Father that will be fine, I'd like to go with you. He knows that Kelly will need a lot of calming down for this phase, so three hours is the minimum to prepare him in."

The next hour seemed to fly by. The sun had dispersed any lingering gloom in the village, and as they drove along the edge of the valley towards their destination, she felt a great surge of emotion at its beauty. Kelly welcomed them with a display of almost arrogance as he tap-danced before her. Even the horse had caught the mood and seemed to know that very soon both of them would be tested to the limit.

As the waiting time grew shorter, so a strange calm enveloped her whole being, as if James' protective arms were holding her close and warm against his body. There was no mistake: her love was somewhere in the crowd watching, and when her name was called, James, Kelly, and Katrina, blended into one as they entered the arena.

Only once had they completely gelled as a team in the dressage phase and that was in practice only a few days ago. Now this would be the second and most important time.

Tremendous applause greeted their performance, and when the scores were added, shockwaves spread like wildfire amongst the crowd. Katrina Chambers on Kelly headed the English competitors, and overall was lying in fourth place.

To say that her rivals were worried would be an understatement of fact. Never in their history of eventing had they ever managed better than the low forties in the dressage.

George phoned his son as soon as the results were announced, and Richard cursed that he had not witnessed his sister's triumph.

James was late for his training, but the adrenaline flowed freely with his upbeat feelings of elation at her performance, so there were no complaints from the coach for the effort applied by his keeper.

At eight o'clock that evening the phone rang in the hall, and as in previous calls it was he that picked up the receiver first. This was not by accident, as he had been sitting with his back against the wall within a foot of the instrument, just waiting.

Usually he rattled off their number before the caller could speak, but this time he hesitated, only momentarily, as if he knew it was not his mother's sister, or the captain of his father's skittle team.

Soft and low like the whisper of the summer breeze came her voice: "James, can I speak to James please?"

He wanted to laugh and cry all at the same time. A

lump came into his throat, choking him as he tried to answer.

Katrina heard the catch of breath on the end of the line, and she knew that they had made contact. Would he cut her off without answering? How clearly could he have seen her marred face today, or was it just a hopeful misguided thought that had given her the feeling that he was watching?

"It's me, I've waited, I've waited so long for you to call, my love." The words were not of rejection, but highly charged with emotion as they slowly rolled from his dry lips.

There was so much to say, but not now. Bursting with tension, she looked furtively around. Gripping the table tightly to steady her shaking body, Katrina spoke clearly and precisely into the mouthpiece. "Tomorrow you will wait for me in the valley."

"Who are you talking to?" Her mother breezed by quickly, hardly waiting for the lie her daughter called after her.

"Only Mary Joe, Mother."

James wanted to ask questions, but knew that Katrina would have difficulty in communicating with other people around.

"Yes, I'll wait, I promise, roughly what time?"

Click, the line was dead. He looked at the handset as if it was a spacecraft, shook his head and placed it gently in its cradle. Then he walked into the living room, sat down in a chair, put his head in his hands, and started to analyse their brief few words.

High above the Badminton estate the police helicopter circled. For its occupants, it was going to be a long, long, day. Thousands of people were now converging from all points of the compass towards the Trials on this lovely early May Saturday morning.

The family were gathered close around her, each with their own thoughts. While they watched the other riders go out on Phase A, the roads and tracks first stage, conversation was limited.

Katrina patted Kelly, at the same time whispering in his ear, "How brilliant you are, yes, I love you!"

Richard checked his watch; only five minutes before his sister started the first of the four phases, and aimed for glory.

"Are you nervous, Katrina?" her mother twittered in a high pitched unnatural voice.

"No, Mother, I feel great. Just you watch me, I shall go like hell."

George looked at her with narrowed eyes. The language was not what he expected from his daughter, or the tone.

Katrina circled the start line, trying to calm down her highly-strung horse. He wanted to thunder after the others disappearing in the distance on the roads and tracks phase A. This was only a warm-up for him, and as she went into phase B, the steeple chase, and Kelly flew round inside the time, jumping the fences superbly, Katrina knew for sure that he was on top form. Now they were along the six-miles-plus roads and tracks course, phase C. This was a rider's clock-watching ride, a chance to cool the horse down after the steeplechase. Go too fast and you would take too much out of your horse for the next and most strenuous stage. Go too slow and you would carry over penalty points into the final phase, into the important cross-country course. Katrina controlled her powerhouse beautifully, keeping their partnership just within the time limit set, and as she dismounted, her family and most of the village greeted her with loud cheers. She was overall leader now, although the placings above her had not completed their rides as yet.

The stallion stood like a statue as the vet checked him over. This was a compulsory short rest period, before the big fences stretched horse and rider to their limit. Out in the park shimmered the lake, and from her vantage point high up on her horse's back she could see the muddied water beckoning her. Katrina felt a trickle of sweat run down the side of her face, and she automatically brushed the spot. Kelly snorted, as he smelt the fresh blood, but his mistress leaned forward, and patted his nose. "Whoa, steady, hold it." Katrina fought to keep him in check, as the crowd near her grew deathly silent.

James was in a quandary. Last Saturday, late morning, was the first time they had met. Their re-arranged rendezvous centred around early evening, so there was plenty of scope to try and guess whether Katrina had pulled out of the event or would come later in the day. Well before mid-morning he drove slowly into the stable yard at Home Farm. The only movement came from the two well matched black and white collies who sniffed suspiciously around his car, otherwise the place was deserted. A short time later, chased by the barking dogs, James retraced his route to the farm gate, then turned right towards the village. Soon the barn came into sight, and he gritted his teeth as he turned and parked alongside it. The dusty soil looked as uninviting as before. He grinned, shook his fist at the dirt, hung the coin detector over his shoulder, and started to walk the long way round.

Much later he emptied his pocket and cleaned some of the Roman coins that he had found. Most of them were gleaned from the high ground, close to where he had watched the girl first approach. Was it really only a few days ago? Laughing, he carefully wrapped the twenty or so bronze coins in one of his two pristine white handkerchiefs, then placed them in his pocket. This small hoard would be a big surprise to his father when they were revealed. Anyone passing along the narrow hedgeless road would see the car, so he knew that his love would know exactly where to find him. Looking at his watch he was surprised to find that it was well into the afternoon, but there was no turmoil within him, only an unswerving faith that his love would come, if not sooner, later. Soft and springy felt the grass as he lay out full stretch, and looked towards the light blue sky, hoping to spot a buzzard.

The light breeze ruffled the tops of the trees, but

closer to the ground he could see the valley shimmering in the pleasant warmth. Within a few minutes he had closed first one eye, and then the other, on the pretext that he would see her more clearly in his thoughts. Telltale flickering eyelids betrayed that he was passing into a dream state, then his muscled body relaxed as his breathing grew more regular.

Only a few miles away as James not unwillingly succumbed to sleep, Katrina urged Kelly into the first obstacle. Some of the fences were daunting, and an alternative ride through was offered, but if you took the safer way it took much longer to negotiate, so the riders would lose time. Anxious fellow competitors crowded around the television monitor, as Katrina, setting a blistering pace, sailed over the shortest route as if there was no difficulty at all. Fence after fence was eaten away as the pair drove onward until, coming into sight, loomed her nightmare, the lake. Katrina felt a shiver run up her spine as the tension mounted. They were closing fast, going at a tremendous pace, much too fast, but still in control. Heart beating as if to burst, and crying out, "This is for you, my love," the two of them rose majestically and seemed to hang suspended in the air as though in slow motion, well clear of the obstacle. Welters of spray spurted skywards as the horse plunged into the water, down went his head, and the rider seemed to lift from the saddle under the forward momentum. Silent and still were the crowd, then a mighty roar echoed around the lake as, from the cascade, the two of them emerged defiant. Although they had lost some of their speed, Kelly made short shift of the other elements, and within seconds they were clear of the water and being urged on by the spectators to other glories. There was no shotgun blast to trouble her, no nightmares this May afternoon, the bogey had been overcome. Now the most important challenge had been waiting far too long in the valley for her, and the time was right to face him.

Katrina slowed the reluctant horse as it still wanted to power forward. They were well within the time limit, but with more fences of a varied nature to overcome and the show-jumping tomorrow, every scrap of energy she could save in Kelly now would be repaid with interest tomorrow.

Television cameras had plotted the explosive ride, and the commentator was trying to give a rational explanation as to her sudden rise to prominence. Other competitors rode by, but there was no sight in her eyes, only thoughts in her mind as she took off her hard hat and balanced it between her thighs. Then her fingers played out and swept back from her face the long hair, plaiting the tail expertly as they had done a thousand times before. Gone was the camouflage that masked her marred features. With head held high Katrina moved slowly almost with reverence towards the upturned faces along the rope barrier. Many called a greeting, but most moved back in awe as she dismounted from the blowing horse. Katrina saw the thumbs-up greeting from her brother, and she wondered what reaction she would have received if she had done what she thought she might and pulled out of the event after the lake fence. But she had beaten fear for her love. The last few days had taken her from a closeted family, almost schoolgirl-like existence into a real and frightening world of blinding passion, attempted murder, suicide, and now the ultimate dream that she had almost cast away. Katrina pursed her lips. No, he could wait another hour, her hero and lover, for first and foremost she knew as a professional rider that Kelly, not James, must come first. This had been his day as much as hers.

Katrina felt the colour flood into her face. Parked against the barn wall was his car. Then she started to shake uncontrollably with bottled-up emotion, partly carried over from her perilous ride, but most of all through her fear of rejection. There were no footprints on the barren soil, and a fleeting smile lit her flushed face as she remembered him telling her how his white socks had acquired brown rings round them the first time they had met.

Although he was asleep, James' instincts registered that the sun's warmth had been obstructed. All his senses went on red alert.

The movement below warned her that he was awake, but try as she would, there was so much tension in her body that it seemed totally impossible to glance down towards him. There was so much to give—every part of her body hungered for him. Would he realise that even her thoughts were like steel?—not soft, but brittle, and she hated herself for it. All she wanted was to fall into his arms and melt into him like snow. Middle finger dabbed the forehead unconsciously as a tiny droplet of perspiration fooled her into thinking it was something worse.

James saw the movement from the statuette figure, and spoke. "Nice day how's your hors—"

Katrina had turned to face him as the first words came from his lips. Then he knew why they had not been together. With one bound he was on his feet holding out his arms to her, and as she leaned forward, tears started to roll uncontrollably down his handsome face. Supple hands lifted her lightly to the ground, as great sobs rent her body.

Katrina saw the magnified eyes searching into her very soul, and in them she saw not pity, only overwhelming love. Gentle was his first kiss on her forehead, then another, and as he moved to her closed eyes, she felt the tension dissipate. Then the warmth came flooding back as their lips met, and with that long and lingering kiss, she tasted the salt of his caring, and love for her. How could he be so strong and masterful, saving her from serious injury, then look on her dreadful features, and show outwardly so much tenderness and emotion? All week long she had put off their meeting, now seeing these other unknown traits of her love, she wished that the clock could be reversed. Katrina let out a long sigh of pleasure, as his arms slipped around her waist and smothered her close into his body. Fifteen minutes later, they were still entwined together; neither of them had said a word for they did not want to break the spell of this very special moment. There had been no sudden rush of passion, as had happened on the canal bank; her love had treated her almost with reverence. But now she could feel the smouldering fire growing rapidly between them, and the overwhelming desire to see and feel his naked flesh almost hurt. High on the ridge close to the drystone wall, they had stood for over an hour, and when Katrina moved out of the clinch, the glow on her face was radiant.

"James, my love, can we go?" The tone was sweet, but there was just a hint of urgency in its utterance.

"Yes, anywhere you like. Do you have to go home?" Question after question flashed through his thoughts as he tried to hide his disappointment.

Katrina laughed loudly. "Shame on you, don't you remember what I promised, are you coming?"

James grinned broadly at her smiling face. "Try and stop me." Bending down, he picked up the four-hundred-and-ninety-nine-pounds-eighty-five-pence coin detector. He clamped it under one arm, and held her close into his body with the other.

Inwardly secret was the smile that crossed her face at his quick response. Close, so close, she could feel his hot panting breath on her neck, and then his hand started to skim lightly over her breast, and down around her inner thighs. She was completely paralysed as his hard muscular body pulled into hers, and his movements became much slower and more deliberate.

Low in the sky the helicopter skimmed across the trees, straddling the valley, whisking a suspected heart-attack spectator from Badminton to the nearby hospital in Bath.

The crescendo of noise beat around their ears as it whirled directly above them on its flight. Katrina loosened her grip as both looked towards the whirling props, and the two of them, locked together, tumbled onto the bridlepath laughing. They stared at each other for a few seconds, then he moved as if to crawl on top of her, but she pushed him away, laughing. "Now! You want me here, in the middle of the path?"

Shaking her head, and pursing her lips she drew in short whistles of breath, almost mocking him. Katrina knew in her thumping heart that any time he could take her.

"When, when?" he pleaded, as she took the offered hand held out for her to rise.

"Do you love me?" she purred, offering her beautiful half-parted lips. Completely forgotten was the damage to her features, and her unfounded worry of his rejection.

"You know I have loved you from the first moment." He paused. "Let me see, five weeks ago."

"Then follow me and prove it."

Katrina moved well out of her ardent pursuer's reach as she led him towards the large copse. James watched intently as she crawled on her hands and knees into a small opening, hardly noticeable unless you knew exactly where to look. Then he followed close behind; there were no sharp thorns to impede his progress, the tunnel had been well used, he could tell. They were in the clear, and he looked in amazement around him. The dense foliage completely encircled an area approximately ten metres across. From the outside the thorn bushes were twice his height, but inside the ground had risen, so standing on tiptoe he could look across to the stream. Sparse fir trees dotted around only partly interrupted the sun's rays, while the short grass and undergrowth played host to hundreds of primroses and bluebells.

This was her retreat, a magic kingdom where you could dream with the spirits of the wild, and, as his love had promised, they would share together their union within its protective enclosure.

Katrina stood silent, watching her love fall under the spell of their surroundings. Then his bright eyes seemed to change colour in the dappled sunlight, and although he never moved, they grew larger and inexplicably merged into a single pool—turquoise, dark blue, green and gold, a large whirlpool, spinning her thoughts into nothing, and drawing her ever closer to its vortex. Click went the smooth button on her riding coat, then another. Shrugging her shoulders, she let the garment fall in a heap behind her. Hypnotised and as if in a dream, she felt the next one go on the high-neck blouse. Swiftly he came to her, and laid his hands on her wrists pushing them down to her sides.

Katrina felt the next three buttons open slowly under inexperienced fingers, then she started to quiver as his moist lips and tongue brushed lightly over her damaged face, then moved down gently from her throat to her shoulder. Harder grew her nipples as each captured piece of naked flesh was invaded, and brought his mouth closer. Then the short stubble on his chin rasped across the swelling mound of her breast, and goose pimples ruffled along her skin. Nearer now, and she waited, tensed for the angelic pain as part of his body would drive into hers. Hot as fire felt her volatile skin, and a great yearning to be fulfilled now was with her. As if he had read her innermost thoughts, her love stood upright and kissed her on the lips. The last restraints were unfastened, and the garment quickly joined its sister on the ground. Seconds later with no attempt to hide from his appraising eyes, Katrina stood completely naked from the waist up. Fascinated, she watched one large finger slip into a gap at the top of his shirt, then slide down the front like a piano player running down the white keys. As the buttons popped, he moved closer.

Almost savagely, she pulled him into her arms, and she groaned as her body was crushed into the soft, yielding, thick velvet grass. Her kisses were long and wanting, and he responded to match her needs. Fire and passion fuelled by the nightmare happenings since they had lain together close to the canal boiled over into a frenzy. Katrina wanted no help as she stripped of the rest of her clothes, and she lay back submissively, as her love made a hash of trying to remove his trousers without taking off his shoes. Down his back the muscles were raised like ridges, and she could clearly see the steeliness in his frame. Dare she peek at his manhood? A huge grin spread across his features as he saw her watching, and with one bound he was on her. Desperation drove them against each other, as if one or both of them might be snatched away at any moment. Katrina raised herself to meet him as he entered, then gasped as he drove hard into her. He paused before he moved deeper, withdrew slightly, pushed forward more slowly, then again, so that every movement communicated a spasm of complete abandonment and ecstasy throughout her responsive body. His chest seemed to push her hardened nipples upwards as he moved deep within her, then they would scream with celestial burns as he withdrew and rubbed them on his downward stroke. The first time she had climaxed before he had entered, but now she could feel how large he was inside her and the tremendous pressure building within.

Great gasps of air came from her lover as he moved more easily within her, sending spasms throughout her whole body. When the volcano erupted within her it was like white-hot fire, as all their emotions boiled over into a frenzied cry of ecstasy from them both.

They lay together long after, both with their own secret thoughts, wrapped within the cocoon of the nest they had found, and surrounded by the overpowering smell of the wild flowers. Katrina was already planning for tomorrow. Home was at the stable this evening and through the night. Then she smiled at her naked handsome lover, whose eyes were closed as if he was asleep, but who every now and again looked across to make sure that she was still there.

Slowly, as the sun dipped in the west and long shadows

reached out over the landscape, the last of the spectators had walked or driven through the gates towards home. The third day of the huge Mitsubishi Badminton Horse Trials closed. Fore some there had been triumph, and others despair, and when tomorrow, the final day came to an end, only *one* would reach ultimate glory.

For the *two* lovers, this was only THE BEGINNING!